NEW BROOM AT ST BRIGID'S

ABOUT THE AUTHOR

Geri Valentine was born in Dublin and now lives near Dundalk, Co Louth. *New Broom at St Brigid's* is the sequel to her first book for children, *Bad Habits at St Brigid's*.

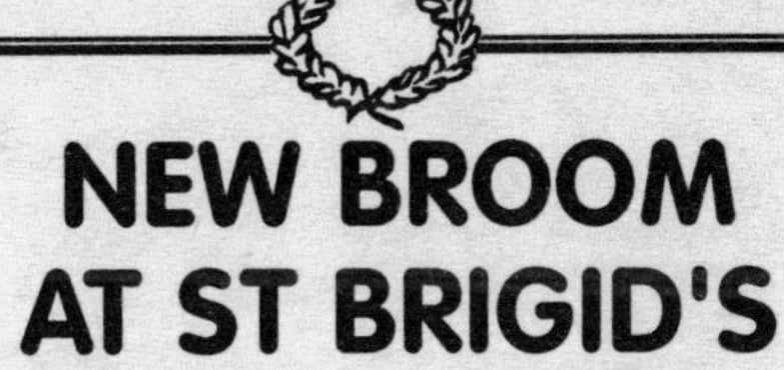

NEW BROOM AT ST BRIGID'S

GERI VALENTINE

POOLBEG

First published in 1993 by
Poolbeg,
A division of Poolbeg Enterprises Ltd,
Knocksedan House,
Swords, Co. Dublin, Ireland

A catalogue record for this book is available from the British Library.

ISBN 1 85371 298 1

Cover illustration by Marie-Louise Fitzpatrick
Cover design by Poolbeg Group Services Ltd
Set by Mac Book Limited in Stone 9.5/14
Printed by Cox & Wyman Limited
Reading, Berks

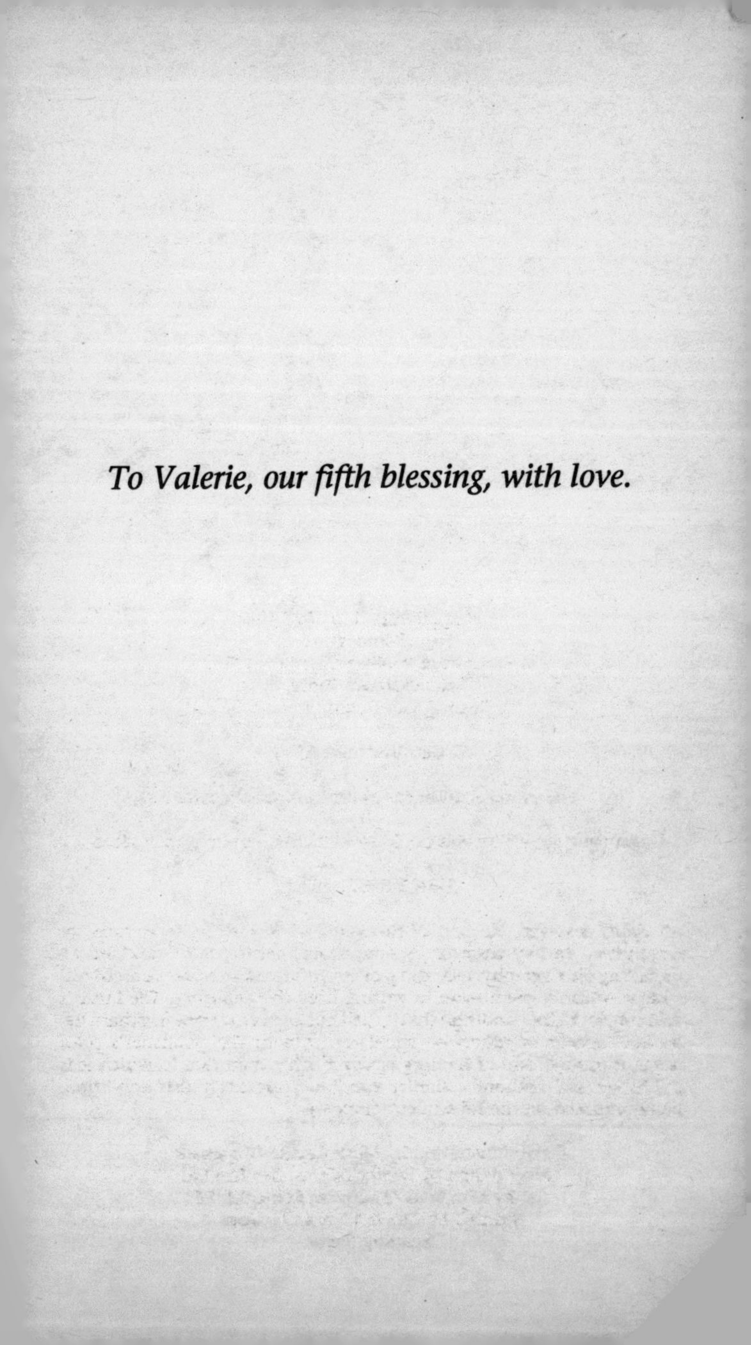

To Valerie, our fifth blessing, with love.

Contents

Prologue

The man in the bed stirred and half-opened his eyes. He muttered a few words drowsily, and then suddenly said in a clear voice, "The twenty-sixth."

The tall woman dressed in navy who stood at the head of the bed spoke to him in a quiet, authoritative voice. "Are you quite sure it's the twenty-sixth?"

The man groaned and muttered again, but when the quiet voice repeated the question, he answered, "Yes, I am."

The woman seemed pleased. She said, "Thank you, Mr Reynolds; you may go to sleep now."

She picked up a pair of scissors and nodded across at a dark, pleasant-looking man who was bending over the patient in the bed. Immediately he withdrew the needle which was inserted in a vein in Mr Reynolds's left arm. Putting some cotton wool on the bead of blood which had appeared on his arm, the woman snipped a piece off a roll of Elastoplast, and placed it neatly across the cotton wool.

"Thank you, Matron," said the dark man. As he spoke, the man in the bed turned and settled himself more comfortably. He seemed to sink into a deep sleep.

"He should sleep for hours now," Matron said with satisfaction,"and he won't remember anything either."

"A good night's work," said the dark man with a smile.

There was a discreet knock on the door. It opened slightly and a nurse peeped in. "I am very sorry, Matron, for disturbing you," she said apologetically, "but you are wanted on the phone in your office."

"Thank you, Nurse Beatty," Matron replied graciously. "I was expecting a call. Come in and look after Dr Waldron. I won't be long." She passed swiftly out of the room.

There was silence for a few minutes after Matron's departure. Then Dr Waldron rose from his position beside the patient and looked at Nurse Beatty. Showing his excellent teeth in a smile, he said, "How do you manage to look so fresh in the middle of the night? You look like a lily, or something." His voice, warm and intimate, continued, "I am exhausted— such a long day I've had. Any chance of a cup of tea?"

Nurse turned her large, soft eyes on him, but all she said was, "What about the patient?" She looked at the recumbent form on the bed.

"Poor Joseph," he answered. "He invents special burglar alarms, really high-class stuff, and suffers from terrible insomnia as well. I have fixed it that he will have a good long sleep now, anyway. You needn't worry about him." He smiled at her again.

"Oh, doctor, you're so devoted," she breathed admiringly. Blushing slightly, she continued, "You deserve a reward for all you do for the patients. I'll get you some tea now." She hurried out of the room.

"Don't forget a nice piece of cake or some biscuits," he called after her, as he sat down in a convenient armchair. He leaned back on the cushions, smiling to himself. He seemed to be very pleased about something.

Down in the office, Matron spoke into the telephone. "Yes, very satisfactory. All the details about the light beams and so on. Pat has settled in well, has she? Good."

As she replaced the receiver, she thought she heard a slight noise behind her. Turning swiftly, she noticed that the door, which she had closed on entering the room, was now open. She stood frowning at it for a few minutes.

However, the silence of the night was undisturbed, except by the sound of a door closing far up in the house and the faint noise of a passing car in the street outside.

Looking thoughtful, Matron left the room, switching off the light and closing the door firmly behind her. As she was returning up the stairs to rejoin Dr Waldron, a conversation was taking place hundreds of miles away, in a convent in Rome.

"Sister Gobnait, I am entrusting to you the cleansing of St Brigid's school and convent," a small stoutish nun was saying solemnly to a tall young woman who seemed to be almost standing to attention in front of her.

"If you remember," the older nun went on, "last

year, Mother Borgia and Sr Mercy used the school for their nefarious activities, aided and abetted by the school handyman, Fursey O'Hare. But for a brother of one of the teachers, a Mr Bill Crilly, I don't know what would have happened to two of the children." She sighed deeply. "It will be a difficult task, but I have every confidence in you, Sr Gobnait. You will leave for Ireland tomorrow," she ended briskly.

"I have my bags packed already. Do not worry, I will not fail you," was the loyal reply.

So began what was recorded in the annals of the order as the Great Reform of Gobnait or, to put it as the girls would prefer, the New Broom at St Brigid's.

1

Major Changes

Detention Room
St Brigid's
20 September

Dear Eithne and Fidelma,

You lucky twins, getting mumps on the last day of the holidays. We're only a few weeks back, and the new nun, Sr Gobnait, is driving us wild. She is known by all as the "Major." The rumour going around is that she was in the army before she joined the convent.

She is going through the school like a bomb. Stiffening us up, as she calls it. She thinks we're a lot of "spineless jellyfish." It's not that she is nasty, as Mercy was, but every day there are new orders issued from her office. She has even given us a new school motto, the three Ds as she calls it: "Discipline, Devotion and Dedication." Nuala's version is: Dull, Demented and Deadly boring. I am terrified she will find this out. Poor Nuala would be up before a firing squad.

Mary Jones is head girl. You know who the prefects are, but the Major has made some new special prees, who are like the SS around the school. You may have noticed I am in detention and all because I was a minute late for study

We now have rowing on the river, and there is a promise of swimming in the summer term. Poor Josie is torn in two; she loves sport, and can't stand the Major.

The teachers are all new, except Miss Crilly, who came back after all. She is taking us orienteering next Thursday morning. I've never done any before, but Josie says it's great fun.

Apparently everyone gets a map and then you go out into the countryside and find markers, which Miss Crilly will have put out there the day before. When you find the markers, you have to fill in the map at the place you think is correct. The one who gets the most places right, wins. I'm looking forward to doing it.

The art teacher is fab. She is really good. I just love art class.

I will just finish off now, as Sr Imelda is looking suspiciously at me. I am meant to be doing an essay.

By the way, I hope you two watch the new soap, Together and Apart, *every day at 1.30 p.m. It's the latest craze in the school. Everyone, even the sixth-*

years, rush up to the common room after dinner to see it.

Love from all, and remember your three Ds, Judith.

P.S. Nuala told me to tell you she loved being a "wibbly wobbly spineless jellyfish" and intended staying that way.

Love, J.

Twenty minutes later, Sr Imelda looked at her watch and let them all go. As soon as Judith got out the door, she made a beeline for the garden, where Josie and Nuala had arranged to meet her. Hurrying along the corridor, she noticed a large crowd around the notice board and, judging from the sounds coming from the girls there, she guessed correctly that the board held another list of commands, of the kind that issued almost daily from Sr Gobnait's office.

She had hardly passed by the group when a small fair girl pushed her way through from the front and, seeing Judith, ran to join her.

"Hi, Judith," she called rather breathlessly as she pushed her hair back from her face. "What a squeeze! I was nearly trampled to death."

Judith turned and waited for her to catch up. "Hi, Aileen," she answered warmly. "Another of the Major's directives, I suppose. What is it this time?"

Aileen nodded vigorously. "Got it in one," she replied. "I was looking for you. Nuala and Josie have gone ahead to Barney, and we're to meet them there."

They had left the castle by now and had passed though the garden to a little wood where they usually met when the weather was suitable. The actual meeting-place was a magnificent beech that they fondly called "Barney." Its spreading branches were easy to climb and it commanded a fine view of the countryside, especially of the River Boyne, which flowed past the school.

As they came into the wood and started down one of its long winding narrow paths, they could hear a clear voice declaiming:

Up from the meadows rich with corn,
Clear in the cool September morn,
The clustered spires of Frederick stand
Green-walled by the hills of Maryland.

They both laughed and said, "Nuala," hurried forward and started climbing the beech with the ease of long practice.

Nuala, hearing them coming, peered down. "Hi, chucks," she called to them cheerfully. "What kept you? I was beginning to think the SS had nabbed you."

Josie moved over on her branch and made room for Judith. "Look down, Judith," she chuckled. "There's a marvellous view of the river from here that will cheer you up after detention."

Judith looked down though the canopy of leaves to where the Boyne flowed majestically by, sparkling in the sunshine. She could see several boats on the river being rather inexpertly rowed, while on the towpath Sr Gobnait, clad in tracksuit, her veil tucked neatly into a large scarf swathed around her neck, shouted encouraging orders in a mixture of Irish and English.

Judith laughed and thumped Josie. "You horror, how could you lure me on to witness the pollution of the river?"

Aileen settled herself comfortably against the tree's trunk and listened grimly to Judith and Josie.

"You won't be laughing when you hear the latest orders from the Major." She sounded doleful. "First of all we have an inspection of our PE gear in the gym at '1900 hours precisely this evening'; any discrepancies will be punished by fines; and secondly, all third and forth-years have to get up tomorrow an hour before our usual time and jog around the castle for half an hour. This will be followed by cold showers and press-ups until breakfast," she finished, well pleased with the reactions of the three, who were stunned at the terrible news.

"So that's why everyone was shrieking around the notice board," said Judith. "I thought it might be bad but not that bad."

At first Josie wouldn't believe a word of it. "You're getting just like Nuala, telling tall stories just for the laugh."

Nuala was indignant . "I like that!" she protested. "I never tell stories. Anyway, I believe it. When I think of how much I loathed that lovely woman, Sr Mercy, last year; and look what we've got in her place!"

"I don't remember you describing her as lovely last year." Judith was amused. "Menace was about the nicest word you ever used."

Nuala grinned. "True, but she doesn't seem so bad when something worse like the Major turns up."

"Did you hear about Gwendoline?" asked Aileen, who seemed to have picked up all the bad news. "Last night the Major found out that Gwendoline wanted a glass of *Jungle* for supper instead of orange squash and she tore a strip off her."

Judith nodded. "I was there. Apparently she thinks that *Jungle* is breaking down the moral fibre of the country,and she suspects it contains toxins as well!"

"Well!" Nuala was indignant. "If she starts getting rid of *Jungle,* which is only a soft drink, the next thing she will forbid is watching *Together and Apart.*"

"Never!" gasped Josie. "She couldn't: we always watch *Together and Apart.* How could we live without the *Jungle* ad and Tara the Teenage Terror!" She looked around at the others. "She couldn't, could she?"

"Of course she could," answered Nuala shortly. "She can do what she likes."

Faint sounds of "*arís, arís*" floated upon the air. The four friends looked at each other. Nuala shrugged her shoulders. "Such energy! And I have a horrible feeling she won't be as easy to fool as Mercy was."

"You're probably right," agreed Judith.

"Who took detention?" asked Nuala idly, as she watched, fascinated, a tiny spider busily spin a gossamer web between two leaves in front of her.

"Sr Imelda, luckily," replied Judith cheerfully. "She gave us an essay to do but I managed to get a long letter written to the twins as well."

"Sr Imelda's not the worst. I hope you warned your cousins to watch *Together and Apart,*" chipped in Josie. "Or they'll find themselves out of things when they return to school."

"Of course I did!" Judith reassured her. "I told them the whole school is crazy about it."

"I'm not," Aileen stated defiantly as three pairs of eyes looked at her in surprise. "I only watch it to see the *Jungle* ads. Melissa and Jason are so boring: always having ghastly unsolvable problems. All they and their friends ever do is yap! Give me Tara the Teenage Terror any day. When she has problems, all she has to do is call for Wrinkles—you know, her pet lion—drink some *Jungle* and everything is fixed pronto!"

"I agree: Tara is terrific," said Josie. "But unfortunately *Jungle* doesn't work for us like that."

"*Jungle* is the brillest drink!" declared Aileen. "All the others are pathetic compared with it! I wish we had Tara and Wrinkles in St B's. They would soon settle Sr Gobnait and her precious special prefects."

"Hear, hear," cried Judith with enthusiasm. "Remember yesterday—one drink of *Jungle* and the impossible maths homework was done perfectly."

"Now you know," laughed Josie, "why Sr Gobnait doesn't like *Jungle*!"

"What a pest that woman is," groaned Nuala. "Imagine we'll have to get up before seven and jog around the grounds! I shudder at the thought!"

Silence fell as they all visualised the horrors of the edict. "I wonder will Bill Crilly take the history club out again," said Josie pensively after a while.

"We must ask Mary Jones," Aileen replied. "She still is head of the club, you know."

"There's the bell for tea," remarked Nuala. "Let's go, chucks: I am starving." And she led the way down the tree. As she dropped lightly to the ground, she said to Judith, who was following her, "It has just occurred to me that all the new teachers are very quiet, ordinary types, just the way you like teachers to be."

"Yes, thank goodness," replied Judith, "though the Major makes up for them quite a bit, doesn't she?" Aileen and Josie agreed fervently.

They soon reached the school door, where they joined the rest of the girls streaming in to tea.

Inside they were met by Sr Gobnait, smiling down at them from her great height. She said firmly but kindly, "Come along, girls. Remember to keep to our three Ds: dedication, devotion, and discipline, and everything will be simply splendid."

"Not to mention demented, deranged and simply dotty," whispered Nuala wickedly to Aileen and Josie, who burst into loud giggles. Seeing the nun looking enquiringly in their direction, Nuala guiltily stammered, "Beautiful evening, sister."

Her attention successfully diverted, Sr Gobnait beamed back at her. "Well done, Nuala!" was her hearty reply. "Positive thinking. Simply splendid."

Fortunately the locker room was quite close at hand, so the friends could have their laugh in peace.

2

Judith and the Ice-House

"Silence, everybody, please." The clear tones of Alison Crilly's voice cut across the excited chatter of the third-years who were grouped around her on the front terrace and reduced it to a low murmur. A repeat order effected complete silence.

"As this is your first experience of orienteering, I have confined the area to the school grounds," she explained. "Now, you all know what to do. There are twelve markers hidden in the grounds. All of them have two letters on them. Study your maps carefully and when you find a marker write the two letters on the map at the place where you found it or think you found it."

She noticed a hand waving at the back of the group. "Yes, Monica, what is it?"

"Please, Miss Crilly, do we put the markers back where we found them or do we bring them back to you?" she asked.

"Just leave them where you find them. This is not

a treasure hunt. Remember also that I will be timing the whole event. The winners will be the girls who come back in the shortest time with the most letters written on their map. And listen carefully: the letters must be marked in their correct places. Now, has everyone got maps and biros?"

A sea of waving maps and a chorus of "Yes, Miss Crilly" greeted her from all sides.

"Very well, then, line up in twos and I will start the first pair off."

The class soon formed themselves into an orderly double line.

As Alison was about to check her watch, she noticed something. "Gwendoline O'Hagan," she said in a resigned voice." Go in at once, and change into the proper uniform."

"But, Miss Crilly, I *am* wearing a tracksuit like everyone else," protested Gwendoline in an aggrieved voice.

The teacher's red hair glinted in the sun. "Go in at once, Gwendoline; pale blue is not uniform and well you know it," she said sharply.

As a rather bad-tempered Gwendoline vanished in the door, the first pair started off, followed at five-minute intervals by the rest of the class.

Nuala and Aileen, who were partners, decided from the first that their best plan would be to go along by the river, across the playing fields and into the woods. About forty minutes later, as Aileen marked their sixth set of letters on the map, Nuala suggested that as they had reached the wood they should have a little rest. "This early morning jogging has me worn out," she said as she sank down on the mossy bank.

"All right," Aileen agreed good-naturedly. "But only for five minutes: we're doing quite well, you know."

"It's due to your brilliant plan, Aileen," Nuala said handsomely. "I'm not really the sporty type, as you know; more the intellectual, you might say."

Aileen laughed. "Not like the two Js; they love this sort of thing. When you were at your singing lessons it was all the Boyne Cup or whether we had a chance to beat Newgrange Coll on the river."

Nuala stretched lazily. "We haven't a chance against Newgrange, though the Major is working hard for it. Anyway, what I want is a good read. It's almost impossible these days."

"It's those special prees: they're always around," grumbled Aileen.

"Too right, mate!" agreed Nuala. "I had quite a good scheme to dodge the jogging and get this great book started but I was nearly nabbed by one of them and I lost courage."

Aileen opened her mouth to answer here but just then they heard a couple of piercing shrieks followed by cries of "Help, help!" They sprang to their feet and ran in the direction that they thought the cries had come from. The sounds led them to a small clearing, where they could see Josie on her knees calling to some invisible person.

When she saw them, she jumped up, ran over and clutched Nuala by the arm.

"It's Judith," she cried. "We were walking along looking for a marker when she suddenly disappeared."

"Josie, Josie," came a muffled voice, and the girls, picking their way carefully, went over to where Josie had been kneeling. Peering down, they could see Judith apparently unhurt, standing on what looked like a pile of leaves and twigs. She was quite out of their reach.

Josie called, "Are you all right?"

"Yes, but I can't get out," was the reply.

"You two stay here with Judith. I'll run for Miss Crilly," suggested Josie. "She'll know what to do."

"Good idea! You'll need to bring ropes, I suppose," said Nuala. "But hurry."

Aileen leaned forward and shouted, "Don't worry, Ju. She's gone for help—Josie, I mean."

"It's quite cold down here," came back the reply. "And very dirty."

It seemed hours to the waiting girls but it was barely twenty minutes later when Josie returned, accompanied not only by a worried-looking Miss Crilly, complete with ropes and a harness-like contraption, but also a large crowd of curious third-years.

"Here they come," called Aileen to a thankful Judith.

"Crashing though the wood like a herd of

elephants," added Nuala caustically.

As soon as Miss Crilly was satisfied that Judith was really unhurt, the ropes were thrown down to her, with instructions about the harness.

They all volunteered to help with the pulling, and in no time at all a very excited Judith was pulled out of the hole, none the worse for wear. But she was covered not only with leaves and twigs but with quite a few creepy-crawlies, causing Gwendoline to shudder.

"You've brought a few friends with you," Nuala observed, as she brushed off some filthy leaves covered with worms and woodlice from Judith's back.

Judith paid no attention to her. "It doesn't matter," she replied impatiently. "Miss Crilly, it's a most interesting place. I know I was lucky to fall on a pile of leaves, for the sides are lined with slabs of rock, granite I think..." she ended uncertainly.

"I wonder what it could have been used for?" asked Aileen.

"To escape from the castle, I think," said Judith excitedly.

Miss Crilly was intrigued. "It might have been a more ordinary reason. An ice-house, perhaps. These old castles used to have stone pits where large slabs of ice would be placed in the winter, and then during the year, when they needed ice in the kitchen, they would come out here and get some."

She laughed at the downcast faces and disappointed murmurs around her. "I could be wrong," she pointed out. "I'll ask Bill; it's really more his line than mine, you know."

"Oh, is Bill still living with you?" asked Josie eagerly. Josie had always been a great fan of Bill Crilly.

Miss Crilly smiled. "He is doing research for a book on Irish monuments. It takes him all around the country but he spends most weekends with me. Anyway, we must get this poor girl back as soon as possible. I am sure you are longing for a bath, Judith."

So the procession set off. Miss Crilly and Judith were escorted by the third-years, who thought it all very romantic and much better fun than looking for markers with letters on them.

They were met at the school by Sr Gobnait, who said, "Well done, Judith, for bravery under fire."

This embarrassed her very much, especially when Monica, carried away by it all, called, "Three cheers for Judith, and let's hope it's an escape out of the castle to freedom." It brought upon her a pained and rather puzzled look from Major Gobnait.

There was great excitement during dinner, and Josie had to tell their story again and again. Opinions as to what the pit was built for varied from escape routes to smugglers and even to trapping wild animals. Needless to remark, the ice-house theory was dismissed as absurd.

When dinner was finished there was the usual stampede to the common room. Nothing, not even finding buried treasure, could keep third-years away from watching the next instalment of *Together and Apart.*

3

Boat-Bashers on the Boyne

"Tara, Tara, where are you?" called an exasperated voice from the open door of an indescribably untidy room. On the floor a mound of clothes heaved and writhed. Out of it a slight figure rose and moved dreamlike across the room, obviously engrossed in something special coming from the earphones clamped on the sides of its fair head.

Turning enormous blue eyes towards the door, the vision shouted, "Looking for me, Mum?"

Her mother came into the room. "Oh, my goodness, Tara, this room is abominable. I'm going down to the shops. Have it perfect by the time I come back or there'll be trouble. I am warning you."

As soon as she was gone, Tara looked around her and said, "I need help!" Raising her voice she called, "Wrinkles!" Immediately, a young lion entered the room, carrying a tray on which stood a bottle with *Jungle* printed across it in flowing black script.

Tara snatched the bottle off the tray and took a long drink. At that the room began to swirl around her, faster and faster. When it settled again, what a change there was! Everything was in perfect order now. Tara sat quietly reading. She looked up and said with a smile, "*Jungle* tamed the terrible untidiness!"

The lion, sitting beside her, winked and purred, "*Jungle* tamed Tara the Terrible!"

A great cheer went up from the watching third-years. "*Jungle* does it again," sighed Aileen. "I wish it would work like that for me."

Nuala, who was sitting beside her, laughed. "I think you have to have Wrinkles for the magic to work."

"All the same," asserted Aileen loyally, "*Jungle* is brill!"

Together and Apart was returning to the screen. Deirdre O'Reilly, the class captain, got up and switched off the set. "Oh, Deirdre," protested Ciara O'Sullivan. "Why did you do that? I only wanted to know what Jason is doing about the party and whether Matthew's uncle was really eaten by the shark!"

"You know we haven't time," said Deirdre, as she led the way to the door.

"It's not fair," grumbled Gráinne. "We never see the second part of *Together and Apart*, except on Wednesdays, and even then there's always games or matches."

She spoke to an empty room, because everyone had left. Mrs McGlade could be very sarcastic to latecomers at art class.

"Where's Judith? She isn't sick, is she?" asked Monica as she passed Nuala and Josie on the long stone corridor which led to the classrooms.

"No, she's fine," answered Nuala. "She was so dirty she had to have a bath and Sr Rosario gave her dinner on a tray. I expect she'll turn up for class."

"That girl is a glutton for news," Aileen said severely as Monica rushed on to catch up with her friends.

"There's Judith now," called Josie. "She's standing at the classroom door."

When they reached Judith, she had time only to whisper, "Meet after school, usual place, have something urgent to tell you!" for Mrs McGlade was already in the room, looking impatiently at the door.

Her mystified friends burned to ask questions but they had to hurry to their places and get out their materials as quickly as possible.

Mrs McGlade wrote on the blackboard: "Theme: Woodland"; then, turning and facing the class, she announced: "Remember form, structure and texture."

With a good deal of shuffling and sighing, the girls forced their minds from various more interesting thoughts and started working.

Towards the end of class, Judith, her drawing finished, dreamily sucking her pencil and gazing into space, was startled by a quiet voice saying, "Very good, Judith. A view from the pit you fell into this morning,

I suppose."

Judith, amazed at how suddenly and silently the teacher had appeared beside her, like a ghost in a film, blushed and replied in a pleased voice, "Well, that's what I hoped it would look like."

"You have succeeded very well indeed. What are the odd markings on the sides of the pit?"

"I don't know, really. The sides appeared to be made of stone. This one here seemed to have a V marked or scratched on it and this one here had a double X on it," replied Judith, pointing to the appropriate places on her drawing. "I wonder what they mean, if anything." She looked at Mrs McGlade hopefully.

"Weathering or age marks," answered the teacher doubtfully. "It doesn't matter. What matters is that the work is good. I think I will pin it up on the board for this week."

"Oh, thank you," said a gratified Judith. Every week, the painting or drawing which was considered the best in the class was pinned up on a special board.

The teacher smiled at her and passed on, taking the drawing with her. Five minutes later, the bell rang and classes were over for the day. Nuala, who had intended being first at the tree, was delayed by Mrs McGlade, who gave her a message to be delivered to an unusually elusive Sr Gobnait.

Eventually, she tracked the nun down, and delivered the message. She was about to leave the castle when she was further delayed by Gwendoline, who rushed up to her, asking mournfully, "Nuala, did you hear the terrible news?"

Nuala stopped, all curiosity. "No, what news?"

"Monica overheard the Major saying to Sr Imelda that she was seriously considering banning *Jungle* in the school. She's convinced it's poison!" she finished dramatically.

"You can't be serious," objected Nuala. "It's only a soft drink—with extra vitamins, I think."

"Oh, is it? Anyway when I told Sr Gobnait that Mummy thinks it's good for me, she said, 'Poppycock, your mother spoils you!'"

Nuala grinned. "Of course she does." And, as she was in a hurry to get away, added, "I wouldn't worry if she bans *Jungle*. We can go underground and have a secret society and then smuggle it into the school."

Gwendoline was delighted and rushed away, saying, "What a fab idea, Nuala! I must tell Monica."

Nuala chuckled, thinking what a funny story it would make to tell the others. However, she forgot Gwendoline when, on reaching the tree, her cheery greeting of "Hi, Chucks!" was met with a burst of excited chatter from Josie and Aileen.

"Look what Ju found in the pit."

Nuala climbed onto her usual branch and held out her hand. Judith placed a small dirty-looking bag in it which Nuala opened carefully. "Oh, Judith, what a beautiful cameo," she cried, then she looked again. "It looks like...but it couldn't be..." she sounded incredulous. "Judith, it isn't one of the missing jewels, is it? I mean, is it one of the ones from last year's robberies that the police are still looking for?"

Judith nodded. "I think so, anyway. I suppose I should have handed it to Gobnait but I shoved it in my pocket and in the excitement I forgot about it. Now I don't know what to do."

"Sr Gobnait doesn't like anyone to talk about last year at all," Josie commented. "I suppose the nuns all find it embarrassing."

"I wonder how it got into the pit," said Aileen. "If I remember, a gold watch was found in a flowerbed. Funny goings-on."

Nuala had been thinking and now she said, "I think, Ju, the best person to tell is Bill Crilly."

"Yes," agreed Judith thankfully. "Bill would know what to do, and Miss Crilly said she would tell him about the pit."

Just then a confused sound of splashing and loud laughter came to their ears. They all immediately peered out through the branches at the Boyne below.

"What a cheek," shouted Nuala indignantly as she watched a boatload of boys, all laughing and jeering, trying to sink St Brigid's boats with their oars.

"Hey, you yobbos!" called Josie, nearly falling off the branch in her rage. "Leave those boats alone!"

The boys were making so much noise they didn't hear a thing. The ringleader, who seemed to be much older than the other boys, was urging them on. Aileen suddenly said, "They're from Newgrange College and that small one there is my cousin David."

"Good," replied Nuala. "Now we'll be able to find out that big thug's name."

Just then the school teams came running down towards the noisy scene. Shouts of "Get back to your knitting!" and "You'll wet your frocks!" floated up to the helpless quartet in the tree.

Suddenly, and for no apparent reason, the boys shot off upstream and were soon out of sight. Major Gobnait had appeared on the scene, directing the St Brigid's teams.

The third-years drew discreetly back into their tree, Nuala giving Josie a helping hand. "Are you all right, Judith?" asked Aileen. "You look very pale."

"I'm fine," replied Judith cheerfully. "It's just this soreness in my side. I think I must have strained something when I fell into the pit this morning."

"You should report it to Sr Joseph," advised a sympathetic Nuala.

"Well, I will if it gets any worse, but I expect it will be better by tomorrow," was Judith's light-hearted reply.

The story of the Newgrange assault spread through the school like wildfire. There was a great variety of schemes suggested to get revenge. They all had one thing in common: they were impossible to carry out.

As Judith was dropping off to sleep that night, she realised that they hadn't worked out what she was going to do about the cameo. To her amazement she found herself explaining to Sr Gobnait that the boys of Newgrange College were really searching for the cameo when they attacked the boats. She confided in the Major, "The cameo has magic power, and can turn the Boyne into *Jungle*. They want to bottle it and sell it for millions."

She wasn't surprised when the Major answered, "Simply splendid!"

The moon, which had been hiding behind a cloud, decided to come out and shine in the windows of St Ita's dormitory. When its beams fell upon Judith's face, she was fast asleep.

4

Madame Nuala—Fortune-Teller

"I am not leaving this common room until the team lists are pinned upon the board," announced Josie firmly. "I don't care what Major Gobnait may say about God's fresh air."

There were murmurs of agreement from all around her. It was a half-day and most of the third-years were watching television.

"Especially as it's starting to rain," agreed Aileen, leaving the window and coming over to join her friend. She perched herself on the radiator in direct contravention of regulations and asked Josie, "Where are Nuala and Judith?"

"I don't know about Nuala, but Judith is up helping the twins unpack and giving them all the lowdown about the term so far."

Ciara O'Sullivan got up from the floor. "There's nothing on television. I think I'll go up to see Eithne and Fidelma and hear about the mumps."

She left the room, nearly colliding with Judith, who was coming in. "Hi, Judith, we're over here," called Aileen from across the room.

Judith sat on the couch beside Josie, who asked, "How are the twins?"

"Fine. I missed Tara. What happened today?"

"She spilled coffee all over her good jeans," answered Aileen with enthusiasm. "Then the phone rang and she was invited to a party!"

"So she called for Wrinkles and *Jungle* and hey presto! she leaves the house a minute later, same jeans, only they look twice as good!" burst in Josie, laughing sceptically.

"Think what Wrinkles could do for the first eleven," grinned Judith, with a wink at Aileen. "That would get her laughing in a different way." Aileen was distracted from answering by the sight of Nuala, who was crossing over the room in their direction.

"Nuala as usual stuck in a book," she said resignedly. "Just look at her weaving her way through all those in front of the television without once lifting her eyes from the page."

"What are you reading, Nuala?" Josie asked as she passed by.

"Not reading, chucks, studying," replied Nuala, joining Aileen on the radiator.

"You studying," Josie jeered. "That'll be the day!"

Nuala raised her eyes from her book and looked in a pained way at Josie. "You'll regret that," she said coldly. "Don't you know I'm the gal with the inside track on your progress? I can tell your fortune."

There was a chorus of disbelieving remarks from the girls scattered all around the room. She held up a hand to stop their comments. "Hush, please. Now, Judith, you're Libra; well, the new moon heralds some change in your domestic life, even a possible house move. Or you, Aileen; Leo, isn't it? Your new moon focuses on partnerships and if you are single a new romance." Aileen looked pleased, amidst a knowing chorus of oohs and aahs.

"What about me?" asked Josie.

"So you have changed your tune, have you?" said Nuala, still speaking in a mysterious voice. "Ah, let me see," she hissed as she turned over the pages of the book. "Yes, yes! Here it is: the new moon indicates that you need shin-guards, to protect you as you fly up the field on the right wing for Junior A."

There was silence in the room for about a minute, then Josie jumped up with a shriek, and tried to snatch the book from Nuala, who held it above her head. "Now, now," she protested, "the book never lies, but you must have the gift to understand it."

Josie, making a long arm, wrenched the book from Nuala and opened it triumphantly. Her face dropped and she said in a disgusted voice. "French Texts and Tests Book 1. What's going on here anyway?"

Ciara O'Sullivan rushed in through the open door of the room and called over to them, "The team list are up and, Josie, you're right wing for Junior A."

"I told you; the book never lies," repeated Nuala, but to an almost empty room, as a stunned Josie was borne out of the room and down the stairs by her delighted friends, to read the news for herself.

Nuala, following at a more leisurely pace, was surprised to find Judith sitting on the stairs, all hunched up and clutching her side. She groaned in reply to Nuala's solicitous inquiries and said, "My side, the pain in my side."

"Don't move. I'll be back in a minute." Nuala flew down the stairs to where half the school were crowded around the hockey lists. Just beyond them she could see the tall figure of Sr Gobnait in deep conversation with the special prefects.

To the great delight of all the girls present, Nuala suddenly emptied into the corridor, shouting loudly, "Major Gobnait, Major Gobnait!"

Josie, who had just turned away from the board, closed her eyes in horror and muttered to Aileen, who was standing beside her, "That's torn it properly. She's for it now." A shocked Aileen could only nod her head in reply.

However, when Nuala reached Sr Gobnait and panted out, "Come quickly, please, Sister. Judith is lying on the stairs in terrible pain." The nun said nothing but walked swiftly towards Nuala, who immediately turned and led the way, taking the stairs two steps at a time.

When they reached Judith, Sr Gobnait, taking in

the situation with a glance, ordered the two prefects to carry the invalid up to the infirmary. It wasn't long before Sr Joseph was on the phone to the school doctor.

Josie was late for tea so she just slipped into her place and without delay started eating her egg and chips. At first she paid no attention to Gwendoline, sitting opposite her and holding forth on fortune-telling. Until she heard her say, "Well, Nuala was right about Josie and now Judith is moving to St Winifred's. It all adds up, doesn't it?"

"What's she on about Judith moving to where?" she asked Deirdre O'Reilly, who was sitting next to her.

"Where have you been?" Deirdre was amazed. "Don't you know that Judith has acute appendicitis and she is having an operation this evening."

A surprised Josie replied, "Una called a meeting of all the teams for a pep talk and she kept us very late. Poor Judith, acute appendicitis! She's had a pain in her side since she fell in the pit."

Deirdre nodded solemnly. "I know about it. Anyway, Dr Murphy was here and Sr Frances is taking Judith to St Winifred's Clinic. It's somewhere near Trim, I think," she said vaguely.

Josie looked around the refectory. She could see Aileen at the next table, but there was no sign of Nuala anywhere. "Anyway, it's nonsense about seeing the future. Nuala was having us on; you know she loves joking," she explained to Gwendoline, who wasn't impressed.

"You're so practical, Josie," she said airily. "But I know Mummy often goes to palmists. She finds it very useful about planning parties and things."

While this exchange was going on in the refectory, Judith was walking slowly down the stairs to the car for the drive to the clinic. They met Nuala at the foot of the stairs.

"Hi, chuck," she said cheerfully to Judith. "The best of luck, we'll all be praying for you."

"Thanks." Judith smiled faintly and, to Nuala's amazement, held out her hand for a formal handshake. When Nuala's hand closed over the hard object which Judith had slipped to her she understood.

"Leave it to me," she reassured Judith, seeing the anxious look on her face.

Sr Frances became impatient. "We have to go now," she said sharply.

When she heard the car drive off, Nuala ran lightly up to the dorm. She put the cameo away in a safe place, frowning as she wondered how on earth she could get Bill Crilly up to the school and see him on his own.

When Judith arrived at the clinic she was taken off to a room on the first floor where a Nurse Beatty took charge of her and prepared her for her operation.

Only a short time later, she was wheeled into a high-ceilinged theatre which smelt strongly of antiseptics. A masked figure looked down at her and said, "Hello, Judith. Put out your arm. I just want to give you a small injection." What a nice voice, thought Judith, already drowsy from a previous injection given her by Nurse Beatty.

The doctor spoke again, "Count: one, two, three..." Then a strangely familiar voice cut across his with, "I hope I'm in time, Dr Waldron." And Judith knew no more.

5

Wicked Ways at St Winifred's

Aileen sighed heavily and thought wistfully how lucky Judith was, missing the recently introduced mid-term tests—another idea of Sr Gobnait's which apparently came under the heading of dedication. She read the final question on her paper again: "List the causes of the French Revolution." Slowly she picked up her pen and started writing about poverty and bad administration.

Vanessa Ryan, the young and enthusiastic history teacher who was new that year, watched the bent heads of the class, struggling with the test. Her mind roved over the events of the term so far. She thought about Pat McGlade, the art teacher, with whom she shared a house in the village. Pat was a lucky find, she thought, always popping up to Dublin and very decent with lifts. Good-tempered too. How awful it must be for her, having a husband who worked on an oil-rig and seldom or never came home! She noticed Monica's raised hand and went down to see what she wanted.

In the last row of desks, Nuala, who had finished writing, glanced at her watch. Only five minutes left, she saw with satisfaction. She was looking forward to the afternoon ahead, as Mary Jones was taking Josie, Aileen and herself to visit Judith.

***

In room 5B at the clinic, Judith was sitting up in bed and flicking listlessly though a magazine. Now that she was getting better, time had begun to hang heavily on her hands. There was a perfunctory knock on the door; it opened and a head peeped in.

"Can we come in?" asked a familiar voice, and without waiting for a reply it called to someone else outside. "Come on, Josie and Aileen. She's awake."

As Nuala came into the room, the sun shining though the tall windows lit up her cheerful face, now grinning affectionately at Judith. Behind her came Josie and Aileen carrying several paper bags. At once Judith's depression lifted.

"Hi, gang. Am I glad to see you!" she said happily.

"Hi, chuck," said Nuala. "Behold books, food for the mind," and she unloaded several on the bedside table.

Josie and Aileen both called, "Hi, Judith!" and Josie added, "Some fruit—and a few cans of *Jungle*, of course." She placed two bags beside the books.

"Thanks a million. Take a seat and tell me all the

news."

"You look a bit washed out," observed Aileen.

"I'm fine. A bit stiff and sore, of course," Judith replied.

Josie threw herself into an armchair. "What luxury! Don't you find it a bit lonely, though, especially at night?" she asked.

"Not really; the twins were in yesterday with my Aunt Pamela. It's a bit boring, but the books will help."

"What are the nurses like?" asked Nuala, perching herself on the side of the bed.

"They're very nice, especially Nurse Beatty. She's the night nurse and comes in and talks to me quite a bit when she isn't busy. How did you get here?"

"On the bus. Mary Jones came with us. She has a cousin or something here and she wanted to visit him," answered Aileen.

"That reminds me," said Nuala. "We've quite a lot to tell you. First of all, we had a history club meeting last night, and who do you think gave the talk with a video? Bill Crilly!"

Judith looked eagerly at Nuala. "Did you give him the brooch?"

"Yes, sir, I certainly did, and he promised to give it to Gobnait. He examined the pit yesterday and, like his sister, he thinks it was an ice-house."

Judith was disappointed. "Oh, no! I was sure it was something more. What was his theory about it?"

Aileen chipped in, "He thinks Fursey hid some

stuff there and dropped the brooch by accident."

"I suppose so." Judith wasn't pleased. "What was the lecture about?"

"Newgrange. He has a marvellous idea of taking us there for the winter solstice."

"What's that?" asked Judith, all agog.

"What's what?" responded Aileen.

"Newgrange, I think you called it," replied Judith.

"Newgrange is a burial place further up on the Boyne from St B's; it's pre-Celtic, I think," said Nuala. "Anyway, it's terribly old, older even than the Greek burial places, and every year on 21 December at dawn, the sun lights up the whole place through a special hole above the entrance and fills it with golden light."

"Gwendoline wants us to dress up like druids," laughed Josie. "She's talking of ordering a designer outfit from Dublin—complete with headdress!"

"Don't make me laugh," begged Judith. "It hurts my wound."

"Bill said he had to book months ago for a place for himself," said Nuala. "I doubt if he'll get us in, too."

"Any other news?" asked Judith.

"We're having our treasure hunt next week," Josie said. "It's a pity you're missing it."

"Not if it was like last year's!" cried Nuala. "Do you remember Gertie and Lambsie?"

Judith laughed and then regretted it. "Ouch! How could I forget them. I wonder what they're doing now?"

"A secretarial course called 'World Sec,'" said Aileen.

"It means you can get work anywhere in the world, where the guys are plentiful of course," laughed Josie. There was a knock on the door and Mary Jones came in.

"Hi, Judith! How are you?" she called. "I am afraid, girls, we'll have to rush. I didn't realise how late it was. We'll miss the bus."

"That would never do," whispered Nuala to Judith. "Think of all the Ds we would be breaking. Goodbye, Ju. Have a great time at home. When will you be back to school?"

"After half-term, and Nuala, thanks a million for everything, especially you know what." With a chorus of goodbyes, the visitors hastily left the room.

The following night when Nurse Beatty was in the office, reading the day report, she was startled by a quiet voice behind her. "Good evening, Anne. Matron on duty yet?"

"Doctor Waldron! What a fright you gave me," Anne Beatty said severely.

"Why call me doctor when we agreed that you should call me Kenneth, or Ken?" His voice was teasing.

Anne glanced nervously around. "I don't think it's wise around here."

He laughed lightly. "So she's on duty, is she?"

"No, I don't think Matron is in yet. Could I give her a message?" she enquired, smiling at him in return.

"Yes. Tell her I shall be in room 14. I suppose Dr Beverly-Morrissy came in this evening?"

Anne looked at the report. "Yes, the patient came in."

"He isn't a medical doctor, is he?" Dr Waldron asked. "I haven't actually met him yet."

"No, he isn't a medical doctor," Anne replied. "I believe he is a big-shot in the art world. I don't really know much about him. Room 14 isn't on my floor."

"Thank you, darlin'," he said jokingly. "And don't forget to tell the boss!"

Anne shook her head reproachfully at him but she was smiling as she said, "I won't, don't worry." Then she walked off briskly to attend to her patients.

She had visited her first two rooms and was about to go into Judith's room when she saw a tall, familiar figure approaching. "Good evening, Matron." Her tone was respectful. "Dr Waldron asked me to tell you that he would be in room 14."

"Thank you, nurse. How are all your patients?"

"I am just settling them down now, Matron. I will be going in to Judith O'Brien next."

"Judith O'Brien. Of course. Tell her that she is always asleep when I visit her. She has done very well."

"She has indeed, Matron. Are you going to room 14 now?"

"Yes nurse. I'll probably be there for an hour or more, if you need me."

"Thank you, Matron." As Anne watched the older woman walk away and up the stairs, it crossed her mind that Matron moved like a panther, and a pretty fierce one at that. Laughing silently at the thought, she turned and passed into Judith's room.

Several hours later, when everyone was asleep and even the sound of traffic in the street had died away, Judith put on her light and sat up in bed. She had lain awake, turning from side to side, for what seemed hours. Now, fixing her pillows comfortably, she leaned back on them and opened her book, which happened to be *The Thirty-Nine Steps*. She was soon engrossed in the story.

A considerable time later, she put the book down and slipped out of bed. She decided to go out to the bathroom, hoping that she would be able to sleep on her return. There was a dim light on in the landing and the building was wrapped in profound silence. She wondered vaguely where Nurse Beatty was, and on her return from the bathroom, she leaned over the bannisters and looked in the hall below.

How quiet everything is, she thought, and then she became aware of someone speaking nearby. "The opening will be on 26 March; three pieces are involved," came clearly to her.

She stiffened all over when she heard the voice, for not only did she recognise it but it also brought back the memory of the one she heard just before she lost consciousness in the operating theatre! She felt rooted to the spot when she caught the words, "BM will do the unveiling."

A door opening in the landing above her made Judith start and, not wishing to be seen, she slipped quietly back to her room.

Thinking that it might be a good thing to do, she carefully wrote down everything she overheard. Then she placed the piece of paper in between the middle pages of *The Thirty-Nine Steps* and put the book away in her suitcase.

The next day Mrs O'Brien came and took Judith home to London.

6

Caught with Cosy

"The discipline in St Brigid's can only be described as deplorable," declared Sr Gobnait to the prefects sitting silently in a circle around her. "I know it's impossibly hard for you people with all the pressure of the Leaving Cert and the need to study—but something will have to be done about it, and soon."

The prefects shifted uneasily in their seats. There was such a look of determination on the nun's face that they wondered what awful ideas she was going to put before them.

"The third-years are a great worry," she went on. "During the half-term break I watched *Together and Apart* several times and I feel that it may have some bearing on their behaviour. I don't wish to mess up the class timetables, so Sr Felix has kindly agreed to take them for fifteen minutes' meditation every day before afternoon school."

She paused and looked expectantly at the prefects.

One or two of them thought it was a great idea, but the rest, who wouldn't willingly miss an episode of *Together and Apart*, were appalled and felt great sympathy for the unfortunate third-years.

The head girl suggested tentatively that some of the best members of the history club were third-years. Sr Gobnait smiled kindly at her and said, "I am sure some of them are excellent but their general discipline is lax, very lax."

She turned the conversation to other things then. A rather silent and thoughtful group of prefects left her office about an hour later. Sr Gobnait was in good humour; she felt she had wrapped up everything satisfactorily.

Meanwhile, a group of third-years, all unconscious of their fate, were chatting up in the dormitory about the mid-term break.

"Did you go to Paris after all, Gwendoline?" asked Monica, watching her friend carefully unpack her silk underwear and put it away in her locker.

"We did, but I have something much more exciting to tell you," answered Gwendoline. "Daddy knows the man who does the *Jungle* ads and he has promised to do one here! He thinks the castle would be a good background."

Monica gave a loud shriek. "We would see Tara and Wrinkles then!" she cried, and then ran around the dormitory telling the news to the other girls, causing great excitement among them.

"Would Sr Gobnait let them do it?" asked Aileen.

"Oh, I'm sure they could persuade her," Monica replied.

The knowledgeable Gwendoline added, "They'd give the school a lot of money for the use of the castle."

When most of the other girls had gone to the common room, full of the great news, Gwendoline produced a tin of powder. "This is a new hot drink that *Jungle* are bringing out soon and Daddy got me a sample," she told Monica. "It's called *Cosy* and I thought it would be great for cold winter nights. We could make it in the refectory and smuggle it up to the dorm."

Monica looked dubious. "We would never get it past the special prees," she protested.

"That's a point," agreed Gwendoline. "But if we planned it well it would be worth a try. *Cosy* tastes awesome."

"Well, all right, but we'll have to be extra careful. Since Irene O'Shea was made a special prefect, she seems to spend her time picking on our year."

Gwendoline paid no attention to her. She had finished her unpacking and suggested that they should join the others in the common room and hear all the news.

There was great consternation on the following day when the third-years discovered that they had meditation instead of *Together and Apart* at 1.30 p.m.

At first they couldn't believe it but when they realised that it was true, Sr Gobnait was described in a variety of ways that would only serve to confirm her diagnosis that third-year discipline was lax, very lax.

During Irish class that morning a note was passed around inviting everyone to a meeting in the common room after tea that evening to plan a campaign of protest. Everyone vowed to be present.

Immediately after dinner, Sr Gobnait, flanked by her two special prefects, appeared at the refectory door and escorted the sullen third-years to their classroom, where Sr Felix, a solemn nun, awaited them.

"Sit down in your seats, backs straight, hands on knees and eyes closed," she intoned. Under the watchful eye of the Major, everyone obeyed.

Sr Felix sat down and faced the class. "Let us be like the clouds, floating, floating in the air," she chanted. "Let us listen to the sounds around us. Let the world's worries drain away, away."

The bored third-years sat stiffly and fumed with anger. "Let us sit in silence; let us empty our minds." Sr Gobnait, well pleased with her experiment, slipped quietly from the room.

"Let us float like clouds. Let us breathe deeply. Relax; relax; r-e-l-a-x." It occurred to Sr Felix that she had never noticed such rigid backs in her meditation class before. She felt that everyone was really trying very hard. Tomorrow they could lie on the floor for a change, she decided happily.

"She kept up that blessed nonsense for a full fifteen minutes," Nuala said later to Judith, who had arrived back just at teatime. "And we're going to have it every day for weeks, they say!"

"Surely every day is excessive," complained Judith.

"Hi, Judith," called Josie, who had come into the common room. "You look marvellous. How do you feel?"

"Hi, Josie. I feel great. Nuala has been telling me about the terrible Sr Felix."

"Isn't it sickening; you should hear Aileen on it. She misses the *Jungle* ad even more than *Together and Apart.*"

Judith and Nuala laughed. Aileen's devotion to Tara and *Jungle* was a joke with everyone. The room was now noisy with everyone present, all talking at the tops of their voices. Deirdre O'Reilly jumped up on a chair and by dint of clapping and shouting shut everyone up.

"As class captain," she shouted, "I called this meeting to see what we can do about the extraordinary behaviour of Sr Gobnait."

"Let's march through the school chanting, 'Down with Gobnait,'" someone suggested.

"Let's go on strike," came from another girl.

"No, no, they're silly ideas," answered Deirdre. "We need something clever."

Naturally, no-one could think of anything clever, and silence fell on all present. This was broken by the door opening and the entry of Gwendoline and Monica, laughing and giggling.

"Listen, Deirdre," said Gwendoline, in a very

pleased way. "Don't worry about *Together and Apart.* I have just been on the phone to Mummy and she is going to video it every day and send it on to me. We can watch it on the school video."

Everyone cheered, except Deirdre, who said, "We aren't allowed use the school video without permission."

Josie jumped up. "Let's ask Miss Crilly to get us a video about nature or animals or something like that. She has a video recorder in the science lab and we could switch them."

"That's quite a good idea," said Nuala. "Perhaps if we were extra good at the meditation, the Major might relent and let us watch the television again after a week or so."

"Well, we'll try that," asked Deirdre. "Raise your hands for yes." There was a unanimous show of hands, and so ended the protest meeting.

Gwendoline was the heroine of the hour and, unfortunately, it went to her head. Despite pleas for caution from Monica, she insisted on trying out *Cosy* that night.

The two girls slipped out of the dormitory as soon as they had changed into their night-clothes. They went cautiously down to the refectory and Gwendoline, producing her tin, made two mugs of the new beverage.

"It looks great," said Monica. "And it smells nice too. Will we drink it here?"

"No," answered Gwendoline. "It's too risky; just carry your mug carefully, I didn't fill them up. We didn't meet anyone coming down, so we'll probably be safe enough going back." And she led the way out of the room.

Alas for the reckless pair! They had barely reached the top of the stairs when who should they see outside their dormitory but the Major, fortunately looking the other way. Gwendoline hissed, "Put your mug in your pocket and walk carefully." They both walked slowly along the corridor. As they reached the dorm, Sr Gobnait turned around and looked keenly at Gwendoline, who was a bit ahead of Monica.

"Are you all right, Gwendoline?" she asked.

"Yes, sister; of course, sister," Gwendoline answered respectfully.

"Why are you walking like an old woman then?" asked the puzzled nun.

"Am I?" was the innocent answer, as Gwendoline, with a sigh of relief, reached the dormitory door and passed safely in.

Monica, close behind her, was so upset by this exchange that she wobbled visibly and split hot *Cosy* all down one side of her pale pink dressing-gown. Looking up, she saw the expression on the Major's face, burst into tears and gave all away.

The next day, everyone heard that Gwendoline and Monica had been forbidden to drink *Jungle* for the rest of the term. Sr Gobnait also put the rest of the third-years on their honour not to share any of their Jungle with the unfortunate pair.

7

Plots and Plans

As she waited for Fidelma and Judith, Eithne went over to the dormitory window to see if the coach had arrived.

She was just in time to catch a glimpse of Mrs McGlade's white Fiat as it nipped smartly down the drive and vanished out of sight of the castle.

"She'll be at the National Gallery hours before us," she remarked to Aileen, who had joined her at the window.

"It will give her time to prepare the place for us," quipped Aileen, who was in great form. "You know what I mean: polish up the pictures; warn McDonald's to have the chip-basket on—that sort of thing."

"I never knew that you were so keen on art before," grinned Eithne. "For a minute I was afraid that you had turned into my cousin Judith."

"No fear of that," responded Aileen cheerfully. "But listening to a lecture on art from Mrs McGlade is much more pleasant than maths and Irish with Sr

Catherine. Then there's a Big Mac and chips to look forward to afterwards."

Eithne laughed. "Not to mention cans of *Jungle*. Judith thinks Mrs McGlade is a terrific teacher; she's talking about getting extra lessons from her."

"Rather her than me," replied Aileen. "But Judith is good at art, and then she's quite the teacher's pet, isn't she? It makes a big difference."

"There's the coach," called Eithne, who had been watching for it all the time. "Let's go down and bag the whole back seat for ourselves."

Aileen was agreeable, and they immediately left the dormitory and ran quickly down to the waiting bus.

They were soon followed by the rest of the class. Nuala, who was one of the last to get into the coach, sank gratefully into her place, between Aileen and Judith. "Hi, chucks!" she greeted them as usual. "This is a lucky break for me. Usually I have to go to to my singing lessons with any old person who just happens to be going to Dublin for the day."

"Poor Nuala," commiserated Judith. "You'll miss the lecture though. I'm looking forward to it so much."

Nuala didn't appear to be particularly downcast at the thought of missing the lecture. "It can't be helped," she replied cheerfully. "You can tell me all about it on the way home."

The driver got into the bus and slammed the door shut. Soon they were on their way to Dublin.

Fidelma passed around sweets. At first there was

silence at the back of the coach, then Aileen asked, "Did any of you hear a rumour about a ghost in the castle?"

Everyone looked interested but nobody had heard the rumour. "Ghosts and castles somehow go together," Nuala pointed out. "But for some peculiar reason, we never had one in St B's—not that I heard of."

Aileen nodded her head. "I know, but the other night two first-years were walking along the chapel corridor and they swear that something or someone appeared out of nowhere in front of them. At first they thought that it was a nun; then it moved and a second later it had completely disappeared."

"First-years!" Nuala's voice was derisory. "I wouldn't mind them. They are always seeing things. It was probably a curtain flapping in the half-dark. You know how bad the light is in that corridor."

Monica, who was sitting just in front of them, turned around in her seat. "Last night two fifth-years had almost the very same experience," she reported solemnly. The listening girls were impressed. Fifth-years—that was a different story.

"Where did their ghost appear?" asked Nuala, still slightly sceptical.

"In the dormitory corridor; the Major is going to investigate it herself!" was Monica's reply.

"I pity the ghost then," commented Nuala. "I'd put my money on the Major any day. She'll catch him or her, you can depend on it."

"I wonder what it looked like," asked Aileen. "You

know what I mean, had it flowing draperies and burning eyes, like they have in late-night films or cartoons."

Monica was busy talking to Gwendoline, so Judith tapped her shoulder and asked her about the ghost's appearance.

Monica was gratified by all this attention and did her best to describe the visitation. "Well," she began, "as far as I can make out, they felt more than saw the thing. Then it moved, and a minute later it was gone, but they thought it wore a hood. Of course they were too frightened really to notice anything special."

"That's a great description, I must say," a disgruntled Josie burst out. "Even Sherlock Holmes wouldn't have stood a chance with it!"

"If you ask me, it's all a story to fool the Major," said Judith.

Everyone agreed, so the conversation turned to other things, and the rest of the journey to Dublin passed quickly.

When the coach stopped at the National Gallery, Nuala left them for her singing lessons, promising to meet them later. She hadn't far to go, as Mr Lynch, her teacher, lived in Clare Street, which was just around the corner, conveniently near the gallery.

The other girls trooped to the front of the building, where an impatient Mrs McGlade was waiting for them.

"Come along at once, girls," she instructed them. When they reached the first room she said, "Stand around me in a group and I will start with the first picture on the right wall and move clockwise."

They all moved into position and the teacher started pointing out the history and fine points of the first picture, which happened to be a landscape by Jack Yeats.

They were leaving one room and going into another when a huge canvas depicting a naval battle caught Judith's eye. She was studying it closely when Josie came in search of her. "What I would like to know," mused Judith audibly, "is did the artist hang around on board ship dodging the cannon balls and making sketches of the battle and the wounded, or did he stay safely at home and paint it all from a written account?"

"I've no idea," replied Josie apologetically. "You should ask Mrs McGlade. She sent me to get you." She turned sharply to return to the other room and, to her surprise, she tripped over a bucket and mop and fell heavily to the floor.

Judith rushed over to help her but before she reached Josie, a small woman in a faded blue overall bent over the fallen girl and helped her up. As she did so, she repeated in contrite tones, "I am so sorry, miss, so very sorry. I hope you haven't hurt yourself."

She brushed Josie's clothes down and patted her hair with rubber-gloved hands, repeating her apologies. Josie laughingly disclaimed any injury. She spoke kindly to the woman, whose anxious eyes looked out at her from under a mop of thick black curls, which seemed too heavy for her little face.

"No, I'm not hurt. I'm fine; truly I am," she protested. "Please don't apologise, it was my fault for not looking where I was going."

She joined Judith and they quickly left the room to look for the rest of their class. Some time later, at the end of their lecture, when the girls were streaming out of the building, laughing and talking, Josie said to Judith, "There's that poor little woman over there. I must go over and say something to her. She was so upset by my fall. You go ahead, I won't be long, I will catch up with you in the coach in a minute or two."

She went over to speak to the woman, who was leaning against the wall at the back of the building, smoking a cigarette. "I just came over to say," started Josie, as she reached the wall, and then she stopped. For, when the woman in the blue overall stubbed out her cigarette and turned and looked enquiringly at Josie, the face that stared out from under the heavy black curls was that of a complete stranger.

She gazed blankly at Josie, who managed to stammer out, "I am very sorry, I must have mixed you up with someone else." She backed away; then turned and fled over to the coach, where she met the rest of the girls.

As soon as the coach had moved away and turned the corner into Clare Street, Mrs McGlade came down the steps of the gallery and walked over to her car, passing on her way the woman Josie had just been speaking to.

The cleaning woman, for that was her occupation,

straightened up and seemed to grow taller. There was no blankness in the long appraising glance she gave the art teacher as she passed her on her way back into the building. Mrs McGlade paid no attention to the woman but got into her car and soon drove away.

Nuala noticed that Josie was very quiet during tea. When they were back in the coach and travelling home to St Brigid's, she said to her, "What's up, chuck? You haven't said a word for ages, even in McDonald's."

"It was that woman, Nuala," answered Josie in a strained voice. "She had the wrong face, you see."

"What woman?" asked Nuala in surprise. "And how could she have the wrong face?"

So Josie told her about the incident in the gallery. "You never saw such thick black curls as she had," she said earnestly. "I've never seen anything like them. And then I came out of the gallery and I saw them again, plus the blue overall, so how was I to know that it was a different person! The funny thing is," she concluded, "I have a very strong feeling that I have seen that woman before somewhere. It's in my mind but I just can't place it."

Nuala was intrigued. "Which woman's face have you seen before, the first or the second woman?" she asked.

"The second one," Josie replied thoughtfully. "I have been trying to imagine her without the curls and I know I've seen her before somewhere. It's very irritating."

Nuala grinned. "Don't try, and it might come to

you. It's a very interesting story all the same. I hope you remember who she is, and don't forget to tell me as soon as you do."

Judith nudged Nuala and asked, "Shall I start telling you about the lecture now?"

"I can't wait to hear all about it, Judith, but I must tell you something first. I met Mary and Una coming from Grafton Street this afternoon, when I was on my way to singing lessons, and what do you think they were doing?" She leaned back and looked at her friends. "They were buying fancy invitation cards for the sixth-year social. It's on Thursday week in the castle, and who do you think they are inviting?"

"I know. Newgrange College," chipped in Aileen. "I met my cousin, David, during mid-term break."

"Did you ask him about those bullies who tried to sink our boats?" questioned Josie eagerly.

"I did indeed and I wrote down their names too." Aileen was pleased with herself.

"Good old Aileen. I wish we could think of some really wicked revenge," pronounced Josie.

"It would have to be something that wouldn't get any of us into trouble," mused Nuala, "and that couldn't be traced to us either."

"Have you any ideas yourself, Nuala?" asked Judith hopefully. "You sound as if you are thinking of something specific."

"Funnily enough, something did occur to me, only yesterday morning," replied Nuala slowly, as if she were gathering her thoughts.

"You know that room, Josie, that Sr Gobnait gave over to the teams. She's terribly proud of it—she had it done up, all spick and span. There's even a brass plate on the door, with 'Teams Only' on it."

Josie nodded eagerly. "Of course I know it. As a member of Junior A, I even have a locker there, with my name on it," she pointed out proudly

"When we all trooped down for the opening ceremony, I noticed a list of names on the notice-board. There you were, Josie, for the week after next, and it made me think."

Josie was eager to explain. "It's a duty roster, Nuala. We take it in turns to see that the room is kept perfectly tidy. The Major intends to hold regular inspections."

"Will you have to salute, stand to attention and say, 'Yes, sir'?" teased Eithne.

Josie looked rueful. "I often wonder about that myself," she confessed.

"I presume there's a point in all this," asked Fidelma. "It's not like you, Nuala, to worry about duty rosters."

"Don't be so cheeky, young Murray," Nuala answered. "I am coming to the point, which is this: I propose that on the night of the social we kidnap the three bullies, lock them in the room (which we'll have roughed up a bit), inform the boss, and let nature take its course!"

Judith yelped. "Kidnap them? Are you crazy: that

big guy is enormous. I bet he plays rugby too."

"Keep your hair on, Judith." Nuala's voice was soothing. "I shall write a letter luring them into the room. Then we'll lock it and let Gobnait loose on them. When she sees the room, she'll skin them alive."

"It's a brill idea," chuckled Aileen. "That room is very near the side door of the castle. Maybe we can pretend to be the spirit of St Brigid taking her revenge."

"We shall be safely up in the dorm by then," insisted Judith.

"There's an awful lot of work to be done on it yet," mused Nuala. "The really hard part will be Josie's: she'll have to make sure that the Major inspects the room before tea, pinch the key, lock them in and get it back to the office again."

"For the honour of St Brigid's, I'd do anything," announced Josie grandly. "Leave it to me."

Judith and the twins clapped admiringly. "That's the spirit, Josie," cheered Aileen. "Now we know Sr Gobnait made the right choice when she picked you for Junior A."

Nuala smiled but all she said was, "Meet me this evening in the common room and I'll write the letter. *Top of the Pops* will be on and no-one will pay the slightest attention to us."

The coach stopped outside the castle and, as the girls were getting off, Monica bumped into Aileen. "You lot are up to something, aren't you?" she asked. "I could hear you plotting things at the back of the coach all the way back."

Aileen looked kindly at her. "How did you guess?" she whispered. "You're quite right. Don't tell anyone, but we're hoping to persuade Sr Gobnait to allow us extra meditation classes before breakfast on Fridays!" And she jumped down the last few steps.

8

Spotted in the Sports Room

"We've discussed the plan; now to write the fatal letter," announced Nuala briskly. She sat down at the table that her cronies had lifted far to the back of the common room, out of sight and sound of the crowd of third-years who were glued to *Top of the Pops*.

Aileen read out from a small notebook. "Bruce O'Dwyer, a big bumptious bully who fancies he's a wow with the chicks. The other two guys, Pat and Brian, just copy him."

Nuala took up her pen. "Is David willing to co-operate?" she asked.

"Definitely," replied Aileen. "He says this Bruce and his two pals are always bullying someone."

Nuala looked into space for a minute or two. Her friends sat down and watched as she started writing rapidly on a piece of paper which bore the school badge Five minutes later, she finished it with a flourish and handed it to Aileen for her approval.

Aileen read out:

Hi, Brucie Baby,

You don't know us, but we know all about you and what a hunk you are. The social next week is going to be a drag, with Sr Gobberletts supervising everyone. So we have hatched an alternative plan and we thought you guys might like to enjoy a bit of fun with us.

If so, don't go to the main door on Thursday; turn the right-hand corner and go in the side door there. Walk down the passage and go into the first door you see. It'll be marked 'Teams Only'. Be sure and bring your two pals with you.

See ya,

Three fun buns of St B's.

"What a ghastly letter!" gasped Judith. "You can't send it. No-one in St Brigid's would write such a thing."

Nuala looked at her solemnly and spoke in an austere voice. "I should hope not. Sr G wouldn't like it at all."

Amidst the giggles coming from the others, Aileen's voice could be heard gloating, "It's just the ticket, Nuala; I bet it will lure them in." She placed it carefully in an envelope. "I'll send it to David and he'll see Bruce gets it," she chuckled.

"Tell him to let us know if it works," suggested Nuala. "No point in setting up the scene for nothing."

"I will," agreed Aileen.

"Put it in code to be on the safe side," was Josie's contribution.

"Good idea," said Nuala. "Something like the 'Biter Bit' would be neat."

They had barely replaced the table in its proper place when Gwendoline came in, all excitement. "I've just been on the phone to Mummy and she says the video is on its way."

"That's brill," said Deirdre O'Reilly. "I'll speak to Miss Crilly tomorrow. I'll say that the whole class wants to see that new video on the Amazon. It's all about rain forests."

"Book it for Wednesday afternoon," requested Eithne. "I know Miss Crilly gives grinds to sixth-years then. Just to be on the safe side."

Sr Gobnait noticed that the third-years were in particularly good humour on their way to bed that night.

Miss Crilly was only too delighted to oblige, especially as the rain forests and their preservation were a pet hobby of hers. She confided to the Major afterwards that she thought the third-years were shaping up very well.

"Fresh air, exercise and Sr Felix are doing wonders for them," beamed the tall nun.

Wednesday afternoon found the whole year sitting quietly in the lab, watching as the camera roved over the Amazon river and listening to a famous voice describe the action of the water on the great forests in its yearly flooding routine. Miss Crilly, satisfied that all was well, left to attend to her grinds, repeating instructions to Deirdre, the class captain, about what to do when the film ended.

Five minutes later, with the door locked, the change was effected and the strains of "Together and Apart, We Nee-eed Each Other" floated over the lab.

When it was all over, Deirdre, standing at the door, called to Gwendoline, "Don't forget to take your cassette; it's beside the set."

Gwendoline and Monica were the last to leave the room. Going over to the set Gwendoline picked up her video, explaining to Monica as she did so that the agony of seeing so many *Jungle* ads at one sitting was driving her crazy. Monica's face expressed complete agreement.

Thursday morning's post brought Aileen up to the dormitory in search of Nuala. "Look what I've got," she cried excitedly.

Nuala took the slip of paper from her and read:

The Biter and the two bit really hard.
Good Luck,
D.

"That's marvellous," exclaimed Nuala. "I'll go over the whole plan at break so everyone will know what they have to do."

"I'll tell the others," promised Aileen with a giggle.

"Whatever you do," warned Nuala, "not a hint of the plan to Gwendoline or Monica: you know what messers they are." Aileen promised and went off whistling to pass on the good news.

That evening there was feverish coming and going between the sixth-year quarters and the gym, where the social was to be held. As the juniors came out of the study, they caught a glimpse of Sr Gobnait, surrounded by a bevy of sixth-years dressed in their best jeans and tops, waiting to welcome the visitors.

As soon as the Newgrange coach was seen turning down the castle drive, Nuala and Josie slipped down the back stairs and stationed themselves in one of the rooms opposite the "Teams Only" dressing place. They kept the door slightly open, so that they could see anyone pass in.

Ten minutes later, as they were about to give up, they heard the sound of shoes creaking along the passage. Nuala peeped out in time to see three figures slink into the marked room.

She drew back and whispered to Josie, "Judging by the strong scent of cheap after-shave wafting across the corridor, it must be them!"

Quickly they crept out and Josie, who had previously oiled the lock, quietly turned the key and removed it to her pocket. As they fled up the back stairs they heard a banging coming from the room. Josie was nervous that they would break it down but Nuala had faith in the weathered oak door.

Nuala looked at her watch and said, "We'll give them about an hour before we start our next move. You know what to do, Josie?"

Josie nodded. "I'll go and get changed now."

Orla McEvoy and Jean Cluskey were passing through the chapel corridor on their way to bed, seriously discussing Miss Ryan, the history teacher, and their chances of getting As in the Junior Certificate. A shuddering, sighing noise coming from the wall interrupted their conversation. "What's that?" asked Orla sharply. They listened intently.

"There it is again," noted Jean. "I wonder what it is?" The noise got louder; it sounded as if someone was moaning in agony. As they stood immobile with blanched faces the lights went out. Almost immediately a luminous figure in loose draperies appeared in front of them.

It raised its arm and, beckoning with one long finger, pointed the way to the back stairs. Its eerie voice whispered, "Come, follow me," at the same time.

Orla screamed and pushed Jean aside in her mad scramble for the main staircase. As she ran, closely followed by the equally scared Jean, she bumped into the rest of the fourth-years in a bunch, on their way to bed.

"It's the ghost! The ghost!" she called to them. "Let me past: it's the ghost!" And she tried to push her way through. The two white, scared faces impressed the other girls so much that a few minutes later, Sr Gobnait, attracted by the noise, was nearly knocked down by the wild, stampeding fourth-years. She was borne up to the chapel corridor, where they were surprised to find that the lights were on again.

Setting her lips in a grim line, she went down the back stairs and was greeted by loud banging noises coming from the "Teams Only" room. Carefully scanning the neatly written lists on the notice-board which hung beside her, she turned to Orla and said: "Get me Josie Cleary from St Ita's dormitory and tell her to bring the key with her."

A few minutes later a scared-looking Josie, accompanied by Nuala, both in dressing-gowns, appeared on the scene. They pushed their way through the big crowd which had now assembled around the door and was following everything with great enjoyment. "The key, please, Josie," said Sr Gobnait, holding out her hand.

Josie looked surprised. "You have it, sister, don't you remember? I gave it back to you after inspection this afternoon."

Judith, who was standing beside Nuala, leaned forward and rattled the door handle. "Look, sister, it's not locked," she said nervously. Sr Gobnait, seeming to swell with annoyance, flung the door of the room wide open.

What a scene met their eyes! There was a series of gasps and oohs and then total silence fell on the watchers, as they took in the piles of shoes, runners, shin-guards and hockey sticks dumped around the room. Some lockers had even been overturned. As they stood watching, three furious-looking boys surged forward, but stopped short when they saw the tall figure of Sr Gobnait.

Nuala and Josie looked in awe at the room. How did the twins manage to do such a thorough job in the little time they had! Judith looked at Sr Gobnait. She seemed to have grown a foot or two.

One of the boys stepped forward. Passing a hand through his untidy hair, he smiled ingratiatingly at the nun and said in what he fancied was a winning way, "Ah, Sister Gobberletts, I am glad to see you."

"What are you doing here?" was the calm reply.

"Oh, nothing, nothing at all, Sr Gobberletts," he answered. "Someone locked us in here, by mistake, I am sure. I must say it's a bit much to be treated so badly but we won't report it to anyone."

"We must be an hour in here at least," burst out one of the other boys furiously.

"Who locked you in?" asked Sr Gobnait in the same mild voice. "And how did they do it? Were you kidnapped, or threatened with a gun perhaps?"

"We were tricked by a letter!"

"I see; so you vandalised this room in revenge."

Bruce answered jeeringly, "We found it this way. You should teach your girls to be tidy," and he grinned at his friends, who gave loud cracks of laughter.

Sr Gobnait turned around. "Everyone go to bed at

once. Nuala, go up and tell the head girl that these boys will be busy here, putting everything back in its proper place. I expect to join her in half an hour."

The girls dispersed, well pleased with the punishment meted out. As Nuala and Judith went along the corridor they heard Sr Gobnait's voice, no longer mild, but cold and intimidating. "Start picking up those shoes and get cracking. I want the place perfect in thirty minutes...or else."

As Nuala was getting into bed, Eithne and Fidelma came over to her, all apologies. Sr Imelda had grabbed them for extra work after school to make up for all the time they missed with the mumps, so they never got to mess up the room after all.

There was a lot of talking and laughing in the dormitory about the incident in the sports room. Eventually most people fell asleep, tired out from the long day.

9

A Shadow in the Light

Judith heard the school clock strike midnight and got out of bed. Hearing movement in Nuala's cubicle, she went over and peeped in. To her delight, Nuala was wide awake too.

"I can't get to sleep," she whispered. "I keep going over the evening in my mind."

"Same here," answered Nuala in a low tone. "I have a few cans of *Jungle* in the common room. Let's go down and get them. It should be safe enough now."

Judith went off to get her dressing-gown and slippers. A few minutes later they left the dormitory and were soon in the common room. They carried chairs over to the still warm radiator and Nuala produced her supply of *Jungle*.

They sat and drank in companionable silence for a while, then Nuala said, "I have a strong suspicion that Sr Gobberletts put two and two together and guessed the whole plot."

Judith laughed. "Sr Gobberletts! And he was so sure that he was wowing her. I hope she doesn't trace it to us."

Nuala lay back in her chair. "Not a chance," she yawned. "I forgot to tell you about Monica and Gwendoline. Apparently they were dying to watch the video of *Together and Apart* again, so they thought that it would be a great chance to slip in to the sixth-year common room and put it on the recorder there, while the social was on." She chuckled with amusement.

"Were they caught then?" asked a puzzled Judith.

"No," answered Nuala. "They were lucky about that. They pressed the button and lay back in their seats to enjoy the sight of Melissa and Jason walking hand and hand on the beach, when to their horror they saw instead a huge alligator waddle across the screen and slip into the Amazon. They had taken the wrong tape!"

"Oh, no! Let's hope Miss Crilly doesn't discover the other tape before they can switch them," said Judith. She had a sudden vision of Gwendoline's face as she watched the alligator appear instead of Jason and Melissa, and began to giggle helplessly.

Nuala watched her with amusement. "Think of what would have happened if they had been caught by the special prees!" she admonished Judith, who began to sober up. "I think we'd better get back to bed. It's well after one!"

They left the common room and moved quietly up the stairs, guided by Nuala's torch. "Isn't it terribly quiet and dark?" whispered Judith. "I feel scared stiff, do you?"

"You bet I do," was Nuala's tense reply.

It wasn't much later when Nuala stopped and clutched Judith's arm. "I think there's someone ahead of us on the stairs," she said in Judith's ear, and then switched off her torch.

Both girls listened with painful intensity. There wasn't a sound in the cold blackness around them. Nuala pressed on the torch and flashed it around the stairs. There was nobody to be seen. "I must have been mistaken," she muttered. "I could have sworn I heard footsteps ahead of us."

They relaxed and crept more quickly up the rest of the stairs. When they reached the landing and were about to turn into the dormitory corridor, Nuala heard the noise again. This time, Judith heard it too. They stopped again and listened, with the same results as before.

They turned into the long dormitory corridor, which seemed even longer than it did in the daytime. Nuala's torch cast only a feeble light here. They walked quietly along and had almost reached their dormitory door when they noticed a beam of light shining about half way down the part of the corridor that still lay ahead of them. The light wavered. Suddenly a huge, grotesque shadow was cast on the opposite wall.

Judith gave a stifled scream. Nuala dropped her torch, which bounced noisily along the floor.

Immediately, the light ahead of them dimmed, there was a faint click and it disappeared completely.

Nuala picked up her torch which, luckily, was still on. She then pushed Judith through the dormitory door, panting with fright. "That wasn't a ghost!" Nuala's voice was wobbly. "Ghosts don't have shadows. There's something fishy going on here!"

"Very fishy. I nearly died when I saw the shadow," agreed the even wobblier voice of Judith. "Was it a man or a woman, do you think?"

Nuala gasped. "I don't know; let's go to bed. We'll talk about it in the morning." They scuttled across the room and got into their beds, where they soon fell asleep.

The next morning the whole school hummed with excitement over what some girl had christened as "St Brigid's revenge on the boat-bashers of Newgrange!" A tired-looking Judith and Nuala paid no attention to the gossip. Immediately after breakfast they hustled the rest of their gang into the garden for a quick meeting before class.

"What's up, Ju?" asked Eithne. "You look awful!"

"Yes," agreed Fidelma. "And Nuala looks as bad."

"Shush, chucks," cautioned Nuala. "We haven't much time; so listen carefully." She told them about the weird experience she had shared with Judith in the night.

The listeners were shocked and excited by the story. "I am glad I wasn't there!" Aileen gasped. "I would have screamed the castle down. That means that those first-years saw something after all, doesn't it?"

"The time was different. And so was the corridor," Fidelma pointed out.

"I don't agree," Aileen replied firmly. "The chapel corridor is just underneath the other one, and if it was seen in the evening, naturally it thought that the middle of the night would be a much better time."

"Which just goes to show, you can't be sure of anything in St Brigid's," joked Fidelma.

"The big question is—what are you going to do about it?" asked Josie. "I suppose you could tell the Major but I don't think you would like to."

Nuala and Judith looked worried. "Apart from the fact that we had no business to be wandering around at night," Judith said, "Nuala feels that after last year we don't know who to trust."

"You don't suspect the Major?" asked Josie.

"I don't know. Though it must be someone in the castle," Nuala answered. "And that shadow was very tall!"

"What about the new teachers?" asked Fidelma.

"They all live in the village," Nuala pointed out. "So do the Crillys. I think we should tell Bill. He gave the cameo to Sr Gobnait without splitting on Judith and we know he is to be trusted."

"That's true," agreed Josie, who always considered Bill perfect anyway.

"How will you get in touch with him?" asked

Aileen. "I thought he was always away."

"I'll have to write and tell him about it," Nuala said, as they started walking back into the castle. The bell for class was ringing and they didn't want any trouble from the Major for being late.

10

Gwendoline Gets the Flu

"Now Judith—" Mrs McGlade's voice was brisk and businesslike. "—make your choice; I am going to Dublin tomorrow and I will leave your picture in to be framed then."

"Thank you," murmured Judith. "The trouble is that I can't make up my mind which one to pick." Since half-term, Judith had been having private lessons several times a week with the art teacher. It was now late November and the result of these lessons hung in front of them: three pictures, each a different view of the castle and the river.

"I'm not surprised," observed Nuala warmly. "They are all terrific." She had been invited to the private viewing, along with Eithne and Fidelma, who were Judith's cousins. Their function was to aid Judith in selecting a picture which she wanted to give her parents for Christmas.

"I think your mum and dad would like the middle

one best," suggested Eithne. "What do you think, Fidelma?"

Her twin nodded her head vigorously. "Deffo! Judith, it's the brillest," was her reply.

Judith turned to Nuala. "What do you think?" she asked.

Nuala looked at the middle picture. Judith had painted it from a sketch she had done in September. The castle, surrounded by trees in their autumnal splendour, overlooking the wide expanse of river, looked serene and peaceful in the sunlight. Nuala grinned. "It's hard to believe that behind that dignified façade, about two hundred of us were shouting and clattering around the place. I think the twins are right, Judith. The middle one is best."

Mrs McGlade suddenly laughed. "I'll take this one then, shall I, Judith?" she asked. Judith nodded and the teacher took down the canvases and rolled them up. "I'll leave the other two in the art room," she said, as she left the room.

While Judith sorted out art materials, the other girls sat on window seats and indulged in a bit of school gossip. "Did you hear that another nun has gone down with flu?" Eithne remarked. "They've brought in a hospital nurse to help Sr Joseph in the infirmary. Her name is Anne Beatty, I think."

Judith looked up. "That must be the night nurse in St Winifred's," she said. "She was great fun."

"The funny thing is, every other year it was the

girls who cluttered up the infirmary, not the nuns," observed Eithne.

Nuala was amused. "It must be all that early morning jogging and those ghastly press-up sessions that did the trick," she said. "Not to mention cold baths. Thank God Sr Gobberletts has switched her attention to the hockey teams."

"Josie says that, despite the Major, we haven't a chance of winning the Boyne Cup this year. They barely scraped into the quarter-finals as it is."

"Ah, well," Nuala replied good-naturedly. "We won it last year. It's only fair to give the other schools a chance."

Eithne grinned. "Josie doesn't see it that way. She blames it on Una, says she's a hopeless captain."

"I know Josie is playing against St Mary's this afternoon, but what happened to Aileen?" asked Judith, who was ready to go.

"She's practising for the Christmas show," answered Nuala. "It's not going to be a patch on last year's of course, but the rumour is that we are going to walk in procession all around the castle in the dark, singing carols and carrying lanterns, finishing around the crib and the Christmas tree in the hall."

"That sounds great!" said Judith. "Do you remember last year and the rubies?"

"We couldn't forget that. By and large, though, Miss Keane's departure has left a hole in the school, hasn't it?" mused Nuala.

"Well, we won the cup last year, without any jogging," agreed Fidelma. "Maybe all the culture she went on about and all that piano-playing was the secret of her success."

"You could be right," said Judith. "I'm ready; let's go!"

They hadn't gone far when the sound of cheering drew them to the common room, where Josie was the centre of a group, all patting her on the back and congratulating her. As they came in, Aileen called over to them. "It's great news, isn't it? Junior A beat St Mary's by four goals to two. They're in the quarter-finals now."

"Hi, Aileen, how's the fiddling?" asked Nuala, after they had shown their pleasure at the good news to Josie.

"I have a letter for you," answered Aileen producing it from her pocket and handing it to Nuala.

Nuala opened the envelope and quickly scanned its contents. "It's from Bill Crilly," she revealed. "He says he will search the pit again and tell us his findings, if any, at the history club, next week."

"Goody, I can't wait until Wednesday," Judith cried. "I bet I'm right and it's a secret escape passage from the castle."

"I agree," teased Nuala. "And when Bill staggers out with the lost gold of the Fir Bolg, I know Sr Gobberletts will pin a big gold D for devoted and dedicated detection on your uniform."

"You can't upset me with that sort of talk, Nuala

O'D." Judith's voice was complacent. "Remember that I was right the last time and you didn't believe me then, either."

It was only two days later when Judith, coming in late to dinner, sat down between Nuala and Aileen and announced excitedly: "I met Nurse Beatty on the stairs just now and what do you think she told me? Hold everything, for it's the news of the century! Sr Gobnait has gone down with the flu!"

"You can't be serious!" exclaimed Aileen. "Is she really sick? The Major?"

"She is. Twenty-four-hour stuff. I gather that she was most reluctant to quit her post, but she couldn't hold out any longer."

"That sounds like her," observed Josie. "She must be feeling really bad."

There was a great babble of noise around the room, as the news passed from table to table. "Poor old Gobberletts! What a pity we can't think of something wild to do while the cat is away," murmured Nuala, as she passed the salt to Gwendoline.

"You think you're smart," snapped Gwendoline. "But one of these days she'll catch you and you'll be in real trouble then."

There was a moment of shocked silence; then Nuala laughed and said, "I'm sure you're right, Gwendoline. I'd better watch my step, hadn't I?"

When it was safe to do so, she asked Aileen, "What's biting her?"

Aileen whispered, "I think Miss Crilly gave her a bad time over putting back the wrong video. Monica's story is that Miss Crilly held a party the other night, and the highlight of the evening was to be a showing of the Amazon video. Amongst those invited were some Friends of the Earth types, and quite a few nuns."

Nuala's eyes widened. "She didn't! She couldn't! No, I don't believe it! Instead of the Amazon, they got Jason and Melissa!"

Aileen nodded. "Not to mention Tara, Wrinkles and the *Jungle* ad. Miss Crilly didn't take to Tara, I believe. Some people have no taste," she remarked bitterly. "Monica says that she was so cross, she forgot to ask Gwendoline any questions about how the videos got mixed up."

Nuala laughed. "What luck for us! I suppose Miss Crilly was jealous of Tara's lovely hair and huge eyes. I know I am. I wonder if she's a horrible spoilt brat."

Aileen was shocked. "I bet Tara is simply perfect."

Dinner over, the third-years straggled as usual slowly up to meditation class. When they reached the classroom, there was no sign of Sr Felix, which was most unusual.

Everyone sat down, chatting in a desultory way. Eventually the class fell silent. In the distance, they could hear the distinctive trip-trip of Sr Felix's approach. Gwendoline, who had been glowering all this time, suddenly got up and locked the door. She turned to the class, put her finger to her lips and whispered loudly,

"Don't make a sound." The surprised class obeyed without question.

It wasn't long before the door handle rattled and rattled. In the silence, Sr Felix's voice could be heard. "This is very strange. I wonder what's happened," and then, "I'll see downstairs." Then they heard her footsteps walking away from the door and so out of her hearing. Gwendoline got up, unlocked the door and returned to her seat.

Within five minutes Sr Felix was back, tried the door again and came into the room. As the puzzled nun walked up to the desk, she could see that everyone was sitting up straight, hands on knees, eyes closed.

Gwendoline opened her eyes, gave a long shuddering sigh and cried, "Oh, sister, you came back to us." Then emboldened by a series of giggles from around the room, she went on in an earnest voice. "You just floated across the room and through the door. I wish I could do that."

Monica, anxious to support her friend, joined in. "Do it again, please, sister." This encouraged some of the bolder spirits to call out, "Please sister, do it again."

The bell for afternoon school rang. Gwendoline got up from her desk and, staggering across the room, fell down at the nun's feet, calling hoarsely, "Jungle, Jungle."

Sr Felix gave one screech and ran out of the room. The whole class rose, thinking that Gwendoline had really surpassed herself. When Monica, followed by

Aileen and Judith went over, they found Gwendoline was really unconscious. Judith felt her face; it was burning.

Deirdre O'Reilly ran at once for help and returned with Nurse Beatty, who confirmed that it was flu. By this time, Gwendoline had recovered consciousness and was able to walk weakly away on the nurse's arm.

Later on that afternoon, during history class, Josie whispered to Aileen, "Meditation class has been suspended for third-years from today. Pass it on." Aileen was only too happy to oblige.

After tea, Nuala, Aileen and Josie decided to go to the common room and play rummy for fifteen minutes before study. They were immersed in the game when Judith came in and joined them. She held out a book to Nuala, saying, "I had a parcel from home and this was in it. It's *The Thirty-Nine Steps*. I am sorry for keeping it so long."

"Thanks Judith," answered Nuala, putting it in her lap and forgetting all about it.

Five minutes later, Judith reminded them, "It's time for study: the bell is about to go."

Looking around the room, which was rapidly emptying, Nuala stood up, forgetting about the book which Judith had returned to her. As it fell to the floor with a clatter, a small piece of paper fluttered out of it and lay at Nuala's feet. "What's this?" asked Nuala, picking it up. She read out in a puzzled voice: "The unveiling is on the twenty-sixth and three pieces are involved."

Memory came flooding back to Judith like a window opening in her mind. She looked around the room; everyone had gone by now except the four of them. "Nuala," she cried. "I forgot to tell you this before but the last night that I was in the clinic, I happened to be coming back from the bathroom in the early hours and I heard a voice talking, on the telephone I think. You won't believe this but I recognised that voice."

"Whose voice was it?" interrupted Nuala sharply.

"I am almost certain that it was the voice of the woman whom we all knew last year as Mother Borgia!"

Gasps of horror came from the girls. "I don't believe it," said Josie. "What would she be doing in a nursing home in the middle of the night?"

"You needn't believe me," retorted an insulted Judith. "But I also heard her speak just before I went to sleep in the operating theatre."

Nuala, realising that Judith's feelings were hurt, quickly broke in. "It would be a great place to hide, if you were on the run. I wonder what the words mean, though. Bad news if Mother Borgia is behind them, you may be sure."

Sr Imelda came into the room, cutting short the further questions that Nuala was dying to ask about the voice.

"Come along, girls," she urged them in her usual kindly way. "It's study time."

They had perforce to go, though each one's mind

was seething with conjecture. They walked sedately enough to the study room, closely followed by Sr Imelda. Nuala said in a low voice to Judith, "It occurs to me that Nurse Beatty would be able to help about the mysterious voice."

Judith's face lit up. "Leave it to me. I'll speak to her tomorrow."

11

History and Mystery

"In conclusion," said Bill Crilly, smiling at the earnest faces before him, "the abbey suffered the fate of all religious houses in the time of King Henry VIII but wasn't really abandoned until 1649, when Oliver Cromwell came to Ireland and destroyed all the remaining churches and monastic buildings. The abbey church was restored in the 1970s and the relic of the True Cross is once again venerated and honoured there."

He sat down to sustained clapping from the history club, a dedicated band of some twenty members who had listened to him with mixed feelings as he spoke, flanked on one side by Sr Frances and on the other by Miss Ryan.

"Teachers!" thought Josie bitterly. "We never had teachers at the club meetings before. It just ruins everything. I don't think I will stay in it if this happens again."

Josie's feelings reflected what the majority of the

club members felt, but Nuala and Judith were more concerned at how they were going to get Bill alone. They wanted to tell him about Judith's "voice on the phone" and also what Nurse Beatty had said—that she thought the owner of the voice was the night matron of the clinic and was called Julia O'Keeffe.

Sr Frances rose and thanked Mr Crilly on behalf of all present and invited everyone to refreshment set out in the adjoining parlour. Then Bill bent over and spoke quietly to her for a few minutes, whereupon she announced, "Mr Crilly has a message to give you about Newgrange."

Bill stood up again. "I am very sorry to have to tell you that the Newgrange outing is cancelled. Apparently they were fully booked up a year ago. I am really very sorry." He took a piece of paper from his pocket and read out, "In connection with the enquiry which Sr Gobnait has entrusted to me, about the pit in the woods, I would like to speak to Nuala, Aileen, Josie and Judith, who I believe were instrumental in finding it. Thank you."

When Sr Frances, Miss Ryan and the rest of the club had left the room, the four girls went over to Bill. "You didn't tell Gobnait about my letter?" asked Nuala anxiously.

"Certainly not. What do you take me for?" replied Bill crossly.

"I got such a fright when you read out that note," Nuala hastened to explain.

"Well, Sr Gobnait asked me to find out about it. I

was only telling the truth," he smiled back at her.

"That's a relief. What do you think of our ghost story?" asked Nuala.

"Well, it's hard to say. Obviously something funny is going on. Are you sure that it isn't someone playing tricks on you?" he wondered, hastily adding, when he saw their disgusted faces, "No, no, I didn't mean that."

"It might be someone outside altogether," Josie suggested. "Tell him about the voice on the phone, Judith."

So Judith told her story once again and when she finished, Bill whistled and said: "You kids live, don't you! You seem to move from one adventure to another."

"I only want a quiet life," Nuala protested, with a grin. "It's really all Judith's fault. Since she came to the school, we've had no peace at all."

"Well, of all the cheek!" Judith started indignantly, but Bill put up his hand.

"Peace," he called. "You know this could be a dangerous business. Don't you think that it might be a good idea to tell Sr Gobnait about it? She seems a decent sort to me."

He wasn't really surprised when the girls shook their heads. "We can't trust anyone in the castle," Nuala explained. "We will just have to watch this end of things and we might be lucky and find out something."

"Promise me one thing," he said in a very serious voice. "If anything at all turns up, get in touch with me at once. I'd feel happier if you would do that." To his relief, the four of them promised immediately.

They were walking across the room as he spoke. Then Nuala noticed that the door, which had been closed, was now slightly open. Suddenly she felt that someone had been listening to their conversation. She made sure to be through the door first, and wasn't surprised when she saw Miss Ryan standing on her own, quite near the door, pretending to be occupied with a cup of tea.

Everyone else was at the other end of the room, grouped around the refreshments table. As soon as the history teacher saw Bill, she bore him off, saying laughingly that she thought he looked hungry and thirsty. Mary Jones plied Bill with ham sandwiches, while Miss Ryan poured out tea for both of them. They were standing a little apart from the others, discussing Newgrange, when they were joined by a preoccupied Sr Frances, who immediately plunged into conversation without any preliminary remarks.

"Mr Crilly, do you know anything about the history of the castle?" she questioned.

"I do," he answered cheerfully. "Anything special you want to know about?"

"Is there any tradition of a ghost or spirit appearing here? Before we bought the castle, of course..."

"Not that I ever heard of," he replied, wondering what these questions were leading up to. She put her empty cup down and immediately Miss Ryan filled it with tea. "Have you had any visitations in the castle lately?" he asked the nun.

Sr Frances laughed grimly. "Well, the first-years have certainly been frightened by something and it worries me. Sr Gobnait thinks it must be the work of a practical joker, but I don't know," she replied. "I definitely thought I heard something odd myself along that corridor one night."

"Now, sister, you're frightening me," laughed Miss Ryan. "I'm glad I live in the village. Aren't you, Mr Crilly?"

Sr Frances paid no attention to this remark but Bill Crilly answered, "In fact when you think of all the awful things that went on in any castle's history, it seems surprising that so few ghostly manifestations are seen." He picked his words carefully. "You know the sort of thing: families hiding priests in secret passages, soldiers searching for them, often killing everybody."

Miss Ryan gave a convulsive start, spilling Sr Frances's full cup of tea over both herself and the nun. "Oh, sister, I'm terribly sorry," she cried contritely. "I really don't know what came over me."

The damage was sufficient for both women to have to leave the room in search of fresh clothes. As they were going out the door, they passed Sr Joseph bustling in looking for Bill. "I have a favour to ask," she said, beaming at him. "Not for me, but for this angel of mercy who has been helping me in the convent for the past few weeks, Nurse Anne Beatty," and she pulled the nurse forward. "This is Mr Crilly, a brother of one of our teaching staff; I'm sure he'll look after you."

Anne Beatty smiled up at Bill. Immediately he said, "I will be delighted to help you in any way." Which created a great impression on the history club!

"Thank you, Mr Crilly. It's just...if it wouldn't put you out...could you give me a lift home? Sr Joseph rang for a taxi hours ago but it hasn't turned up."

"Of course I will, but only on condition you call me Bill," he answered, ushering her out of the room, quite forgetting the members of the history club. Sr Joseph went to see them off.

Nuala and Judith were delighted about the meeting between Bill and Anne. "She would be just perfect for Bill," said Judith enthusiastically, as she helped Nuala to carry the used cups and saucers to the trolley.

"Especially after his bad experience last year," agreed Nuala. "Anyway it will give him a chance to ask her questions about St Winifred's and the peculiar night matron."

Only Josie had reservations. She confided in Aileen that everyone knew that nurses were terribly hard and tough. "Oh, I don't know," Aileen replied. "Judith said she was very good to her. Maybe she's the exception that proves the rule; you know that rule that Sr Imelda is always going on about."

Josie silently loaded the trolley with cutlery and glasses and decided to keep her thoughts to herself in future.

The next day, Friday, the weather changed,

bringing showers of rain and sleet. In the morning, Sr Gobnait, now fully restored to health, informed Nuala that Mrs McGlade had kindly agreed to give her a lift to Dublin for her final singing lesson of the term.

As it was the first week of December, the city was crowded with Christmas shoppers. The heavy traffic delayed their return journey so much that it was almost six-thirty before Mrs McGlade dropped Nuala at the door of the castle, before continuing on her way to her own house in the village.

Nuala was met by Josie and Aileen, who danced out to meet her, full of news of the Christmas rehearsal they had attended in her absence that afternoon. "And when we all stood around the crib, at the end of the procession, Sr Gobnait announced that Nuala O'Donnell would sing 'Holy Night' solo on the big day." Aileen gave Nuala this important news in the cloakroom as she was changing her shoes.

"Did she indeed!" fumed Nuala, who was both tired and hungry. "She might have asked me first. I am so fed up with that woman." And with that she banged her shoes into her locker quite viciously.

Nuala was usually so good-tempered that Aileen paid little attention to her remarks, and tactlessly went on about the rehearsal. Eventually, Nuala could stand no more of it. "Aileen, go and take your grinning friend with you," she ordered. "I don't want to see you two ever again in this world, or the next."

"What's the matter, Nuala?" asked Josie, delicately

omitting any reference to being called "your grinning friend."

"Just go!" reiterated Nuala. "I've had a foul day. Mr Lynch was in awful humour and then I had to put up with that ghastly witch, McGlade, who made me carry piles of paintings and heavy art goods miles to her beastly car. Worst of all, I'm starving."

Judith appeared in the doorway. "Sr Rosario sent me to tell you that that she kept a special tea for you." She grinned at Nuala. "I think you need it."

"She certainly does. Imagine telling me, her oldest friend, to go and leave her alone!" Aileen stumped crossly out of the room, coming back and calling from the door a minute later. "I wouldn't mind so much *this* world, but she included the next one too."

When Nuala arrived up in the common room after a good tea, she was full of apologies to Aileen. "I don't know what came over me, but Mrs McGlade was really a pain. And the number of questions she asked me about everything. By the way, Judith, we got your painting; it's in the art room all wrapped up."

Judith went off to the art room and when she returned, Nuala was telling the others about the crowds in the city. "That reminds me," she said, when she saw Judith. "I bumped into a friend of yours in Dublin today. Nurse Anne Beatty. She was asking for you."

Judith was interested. "Was she on her own?" she asked.

"No, she was hanging on the arm of a well-dressed

man, whom she introduced to me as Dr Waldron. She said he gave you the anaesthetic for your appendix operation."

"I don't remember him at all. What was he like?" asked Judith.

"Well, I didn't take to him much. He just flashed his teeth at me, and mumbled something. They seemed very close. Poor Bill."

Josie gave a short laugh. "You can't say I didn't warn you," she pointed out. "Nurses are tough and he *is* a doctor, after all."

They could hear the bell for study ringing. "I don't believe it," replied Judith loyally as they left the room. "Nurse Anne Beatty isn't like that."

12

Nabbed by Nuala

"Hi, chucks!" greeted Nuala, coming on the last night of term into the common room, where most of the year were busy making lanterns out of cardboard, crêpe paper and torches. She looked around and asked, "Is there any red crêpe paper left? I want to cover my torch for the great carol festival tomorrow."

"Sr Gobnait sees it as a team effort, getting Christmas started in the proper Christian spirit," reproved Judith, as she pushed over a piece of the requested paper.

"It doesn't matter what it is," observed Aileen. "It won't be half as good as last year, when the wise men wore real rubies worth thousands of pounds."

"The pity is that none of us knew that they were rubies," replied Josie grinning. "We all thought that they were plastic from a pound shop."

"Ah," sighed Aileen. "No one could put a show on like Miss Keane."

The others all agreed. Miss Keane was becoming a legend in St Brigid's, particularly since the first eleven were not doing well in the Boyne Cup.

"Surely you mean the Signora Fioretti?" said Nuala. "I often wonder if she wears the boots in Italy. I must get Gwendoline to check." Gwendoline had gone home early because of her flu. Nuala finished decorating her torch and stood back to admire her handiwork.

"I heard the Major tell the prefects to draw all the curtains in the castle. We'll be really in the dark tomorrow," Eithne informed the room.

"We're going to look awesome," remarked Josie with relish, looking at all the homemade lanterns.

The following morning the school, having wound its way around a castle illuminated only by lanterns and torches, came to a stop at the crib in the main hall. Sr Gobnait, looking at the serried rows of girls around the crib and up the stairs onto the first landing, thought the same as Josie, though awesome wasn't the word that came to her mind.

Nuala's singing of "Holy Night" impressed even her friends. Under the cover of the applause, Aileen whispered to Josie, who was standing beside her on the stairs, "It's good to know that Nuala's dad hasn't been wasting his money."

"Especially as old Lynch, the singing teacher, is supposed to charge a bomb for lessons," Josie replied with a giggle.

Sr Gobnait wished the school a Happy Christmas,

and everyone rushed off to change and get ready to go home. Most people were gone by one o'clock and very few sat down to the dinner of sausages and chips, followed by choc-ices. While the girls were in the refectory, Sr Gobnait went to her room, changed into her black tracksuit and draped a towel around her neck. Meeting Sr Frances on the stairs, she informed her that she was going to the gym for a thorough work-out.

Dinner didn't take long and Nuala and Judith, who were expecting Nuala's mother to collect them about three, decided to get all their bags together and leave them beside the main door. First of all they went over to the art room to collect the precious painting, which Judith was taking home for her parents' Christmas present. "Now we're all ready, except for my wash things," Nuala said with quiet satisfaction. "I'll go up and get them now."

"I'll go with you. Look what I've brought from the art room by mistake." Judith, sounding annoyed, held up a large tube of black paint. "I'll leave it in the dorm."

The two girls walked up the stairs, chatting happily about holidays and presents. As they reached the landing, they both heard the peculiar noise again, the same they had heard on the night of the sixth-year social.

This time Nuala suggested, "Let's go along and watch where we saw the light last time. If we're very quiet, we might even catch a glimpse of the ghost."

Judith agreed. "We might be lucky. I'd give a lot to know who it is."

The two girls moved quickly into the corridor. It was pitch-dark there, as the heavy curtains, which had been pulled across the windows for the procession, were still in place. They took up their position, just past the dormitory door, where they had seen the light before.

As they nervously waited with thumping hearts and clammy hands, they were unaware that Sr Gobnait, having finished in the gym, was swiftly mounting the back stairs, on her way up to check the dormitories.

She turned into the dormitory corridor, and suddenly felt that she wasn't alone. Thinking furiously, she stopped and then moved cautiously forward, making no noise in her runners. As she crept along, she heard a click, then a thin pencil of light wavered across the floor in front of her. In its faint glow, a figure could be seen, stepping gingerly out of an aperture in the wall.

From their vantage point, Nuala and Judith observed this action also.

Simultaneously, Nuala and Sr Gobnait launched themselves in a flying leap at the hole in the wall, colliding painfully in mid-air and knocking each other to the ground. Instantly, Sr Gobnait threw the towel around what she imagined was the intruder's neck and Nuala screamed loudly. Judith, hearing Nuala's scream, muttered a prayer, closed her eyes and threw herself forward onto the bodies on the floor, unaware that she was spraying black paint everywhere, on them, the floor and the walls. In the subsequent noise and confusion none of them heard the wall click again and the light disappear.

Sr Frances, walking sedately up the stairs a little later, was horrified to hear shouts, grunts and banging noises coming from the dormitory corridor. For a minute, she hesitated. The thought crossed her mind that the castle had been invaded by poltergeists. However, she knew her duty and, stepping forward, she switched on all the lights, at the same time saying in an icy voice: "Pray, what is going on here?"

Judith and Nuala had by this time gained mastery of the so-called ghost. When the light flooded the corridor, it revealed Nuala sitting heavily on Sr Gobnait's legs and Judith lying across one of her arms.

Nuala, overexcited by the whole event and dazzled by the sudden light, shouted to Sr Frances, "I have him! I've got him and just look at that: he's blacked his face so we shouldn't see him in the dark!"

Judith raised herself up and silently looked in horror at the blackened face in front of her. Sr Frances walked smartly over to see the villain for herself, this evil one who had terrorised all the poor first-years. She gazed at the captive pinned down by the brave third-years and screamed, "It's Sr Gobnait!" and tottered to the stairs, calling for help.

Perhaps it was the work-out followed by the scrimmage in the dark, but Sr Gobnait's spirit was weakened. Though she spoke freely of what she thought of their behaviour, especially the black paint all over the walls, her words were uttered without much conviction and she soon went off to her room.

Mrs O'Donnell arrived just as Judith and Nuala had finished cleaning themselves up. Nuala got into the car beside her mother and announced indignantly, "That's a bit thick, I must say: any decent school would have given us a medal at least. As for that story of hers, I don't believe a word of it, do you, Judith?"

"No, I don't," Judith replied, with conviction. "Didn't we see her step out of that hole in the wall, dressed in a black tracksuit? I wonder what she was doing there."

"Who and what stepped out of where?" asked a bewildered Mrs O'Donnell, as she drove out the school gate.

"It's like this, Mum," Nuala replied. "All this term, we had a ghost stepping out of a hole in the wall, frightening first-years. Now today, when Judith and I were going up to the dorm, we heard the weird noise again and then we went into the corridor, which was pitch-dark, and saw what we took to be the ghost stepping calmly out of the wall. So we jumped it—and who do you think it was all the time but Sr Gobnait, with a black face?" ended Nuala triumphantly.

"I think the black face was my fault," explained Judith. "And of course, she denied everything too."

Mrs O'Donnell reflected with a sigh that this must be the generation gap people were always talking about. "In my day," she observed, "nuns did not step out of holes in walls, dressed in black tracksuits and with blackened faces, disguised as ghosts."

Nuala laughed indulgently. "That was a long time ago but I'm glad to hear it. It gave us a terrible fright. We must ring the others, Ju, and tell them about it."

"Good idea," agreed Judith, who was going to stay with Nuala for a few days before returning to England for Christmas.

13

Major Upheavals

"First night of term is always the same, isn't it, Aileen?" commented Nuala. "Idiots rushing up and down the stairs, shouting excitedly about the holidays, while the rest of us pack-horses drag our goods to the dorms."

Aileen looked at the bags and books at their feet. "It's about time they put a lift in this place," she grumbled, picking up a large soft toy panda and putting it under one arm.

"They're afraid it would destroy the mediaeval character of the castle," answered Nuala sarcastically. She pulled Aileen to one side, as, with cries of "Make way; make way," two girls holding a sheet between them, laden with bed linen and towels, staggered laughingly past them and up the stairs.

Nuala bent down and picked up two bags and an armful of books. "Let's go, or we won't have our cubes fixed up in time."

"Right you are. Lead on," answered Aileen, as she

picked up her own belongings.

They had hardly reached the first landing when an excited Judith, closely followed by Josie, flew down the stairs and greeted them with, "Have you heard the terrible news?"

"Hi, chucks!" replied Nuala, stopping and dropping her burdens to the floor. "Whatever are you talking about."

Josie and Judith answered together. "The dormitory changes! Sr Gobnait has split us all up and we're all scattered around the other dorms."

A horrified Aileen gasped! "You can't be serious, Why did she do that?"

Josie shook her ponytail. "We don't know. You're in St Ita's. I'm in St Catherine's."

"I think I know why she did it," suggested Judith. "She doesn't want us to catch her again popping out of that wall, so she separated us. Of course she changed everyone else around as well, so it wouldn't look obvious."

"So that's what we get for being responsible and caring, risking our lives maybe," Nuala said bitterly. "Well, the next time it happens, the walls can be oozing with people stepping out of all the holes in them, like fat spiders. I shall pass by and pretend not to notice one of them."

Josie laughed. "That'll teach her, but all the same you can see her point of view. I nearly died laughing when you rang up and told me about jumping on her."

Nuala, who had been looking very annoyed, began to smile. "I suppose it *is* funny, but at the time it certainly didn't seem so. It took me the whole of the holidays to get over the shock of it."

Judith agreed fervently. "It was the same for me. I still feel dizzy when I remember looking into that ghastly black face and finding that it was the Major's."

Nuala started to pick up her stuff again. "I'd better get up to the dorm, chucks. Which one is it?" she asked.

"It's St Dympna's. I'll give you a hand," offered Judith, picking up some books.

"I'll do likewise for Aileen," suggested Josie, and they all started up the stairs.

When they reached the dormitory, they were met by doleful Gwendoline. "We are the only third-years in the dorm," she complained. "All the others are fourth-years. When I complained to Sr Gobnait, she only smiled in a superior way and said that she hoped we would benefit from their good example."

"Fourth-years, good example!" expostulated Nuala. "Some of them are swots all right, but the rest spend their time talking about one thing—guys, guys, guys!" And she swept into her cubicle feeling quite murderous.

As she finished making her bed and hanging up her clothes, she heard Monica coming into the dormitory. She wasn't surprised to hear shouts of,"Gwenny, your tan is simply out of this world, super in fact. Where did you go for Christmas?"

Gwendoline laughed pleasantly. "Only the

Caribbean. Come on down to the common room. I have loads to tell you."

Judith made an expressive face as they left the room whispering and giggling. "The only consolation is that I shall have a lot of time for reading in bed this term," remarked Nuala, coming out of her cubicle and taking her books from Judith.

"You brought back enough," said Judith. "I'd like to read *The Hobbit*. Is it good?"

Nuala smacked her lips. "Is it good? It's 'simply splendid!'" She opened the dormitory door and as they passed through she joked, "I'm reading an Agatha Christie at present, where a group of people get together and stab a baddie on a train. It's given me a great idea for a thriller called *Death on the Boyne*."

Judith looked puzzled for a minute and then said with a laugh, "No prizes, I suppose, for the one who guesses the name of the victim."

When they reached the common room, they found it full of third-years, all loudly complaining of the dormitory changes. They were there only a short time when Josie and Aileen appeared full of the latest news. Aileen announced to the room at large, "Sr Gobnait has written a school song called, if you don't mind, 'St Brigid's the Beautiful'!"

"How do you know?" asked Monica.

"You all know Gráinne's sister, Mary, who is a prefect? Well, when Sr Gobnait had all the prefects in for the usual back-to-school pep talk on the three Ds, she told them about the song. Mary leaked the story to Gráinne and she leaked it to us."

"What do we want with a school song?" grumbled Nuala.

"So that when we haul the flag down from the castle battlements at sunset, Nuala O'D can sing it solo and bring tears to our eyes," improvised Josie wickedly.

"Only that I'm so exhausted with the effort of returning to this crazy joint, I would get up and cosh you, Josie," Nuala threatened, amidst the laughter which greeted Josie's remark. "No power on earth could get me to sing solo a song called 'St Brigid's the Beautiful.' Not that I believe that there *is* any song."

"Ha ha, you say that now, but what about a bit of blackmail from the Major?" teased Josie. "What price black paint, for instance?"

"What's that about black paint?" asked Monica eagerly. She suspected that something was going on and she hated to be left out of anything.

"Nothing, Monica, nothing," replied Nuala airily. "It's just that since Josie got into Junior A, I am afraid she has got so big-headed, it might be necessary to throw black paint at her, to reduce the swelling of course."

Monica was amazed. "Sr Gobnait would murder you if you threw black paint at anyone," she pointed out.

"She did...I mean...she would, wouldn't she?" stammered Nuala. "We're only teasing you, Monica. Don't you know *Black Paint* is the very latest and most expensive scent on the market?"

"Is it really?" Monica got up and looked around the room. "I wonder where Gwendoline is. I must ask her if her mother has got it yet." And she bustled out of the room.

"Josie, how could you—in front of Monica? You know what an awful gossip she is," Nuala said seriously.

Josie was contrite. "I forgot about that, but I can't help laughing, when I think of you and Judith in your role of ghostbusters," she chuckled.

Aileen joined them. "Isn't it great news about the swimming pool!" she said as she sat down.

Nuala looked blank. "What news?" she asked.

Aileen was surprised. "Weren't you listening when I told the others? Sr Gobnait told the prefects that they're starting to build it next week so as to be ready for the summer term."

Nuala whistled. "What?" she cried. "It will cost a fortune. Where did they get the dosh from?"

"What were the two of you up to?" asked Aileen crossly. "Josie knows as well as I do that Miss Keane's husband, Signor Fioretti, launched the swimming pool fund with a big cheque. The past pupils chipped in too, and I'm sure there were others who gave as well."

"Sister Gobnait is crazy for St Brigid's to be the top school in the country, in sport and study too, I hear," chipped in Judith.

"That's true," agreed Josie. "Gráinne says Mary was full of hints about more changes but the only definite thing she could get out of her was that a special tennis coach was coming next term."

Nuala groaned. "I knew it. I don't trust Sr Gobnait at all: not only is she too much like the three Ds herself, but there is that little matter of her wandering around inside the castle walls, jumping out on us and then simply denying the whole thing when she was caught." She shrugged her shoulders significantly. "What is she up to, I ask you?"

"It just shows, you can't trust any of them," remarked Josie firmly, if somewhat vaguely.

"There must be some reason for dividing us up too," chipped in Aileen. "We've always shared the same dorm before."

"Probably thinks Nuala and Ju are on to her little game," suggested Josie cheerfully. "I'd be careful, you two! And I wouldn't hang around on your own in the dormitory corridor any more."

Nuala snorted. "Don't be an idiot, Josie," but before she could finish what she was going to say, the common room door opened and the tall figure of Sr Gobnait appeared before them. Nuala felt herself blushing as she remembered the events of the last day of the previous term. She looked across at Judith and wasn't surprised to see that she was equally embarrassed.

"The bell is about to ring, girls," announced Sr Gobnait to the now silent room. "So I will be brief. I came to warn all of you that I won't permit any loose talk going around the school—about anything. The walls have ears and certain people would need to take care!" She looked around the room and asked sharply: "Where are Monica and Gwendoline?"

"I think they are down phoning," replied Deirdre O'Reilly.

The bell went then so Sr Gobnait left and the girls started going to bed. As they walked up the stairs, Judith said in a pleased voice, "Well, at least we know now what the Major was doing in the castle walls!"

"Listening to loose talk, do you mean?" asked Josie.

"I wouldn't have thought that she was that sort," mused Nuala. "It sounds a bit deceitful, devious and downright deadly for her."

"Well," said Aileen, "she was the one who said it, after all, wasn't she?" And everybody had to agree with her.

14

Sinister Surprises

The following Monday morning, Miss Ryan came briskly into the third-year class room. Placing her books on the desk, she stood in front of the class and said, "Good morning, girls. Sit down. I have something very important to say to you."

The surprised third-years pulled out their chairs and noisily sat down, wondering what they were about to hear. When there was complete silence the teacher went on, "Sister Gobnait held a staff conference last night and one of the things she said was that you people have a lot of untapped talent. She wants me to tap it; so for starters everyone is to enter the Celtic Heritage Year essay competition."

"But Miss Ryan," protested Aileen, "we've never had to enter a competition before."

"Well, it's about time you did," was the teacher's calm reply. "You know, Aileen, you and a few others will have to pull your socks up. Sr Gobnait has no time for slackers."

While the class digested this sinister remark, Miss Ryan gave Deirdre entry forms to hand out. "Has everyone got one? Good! The essay must be based on an event or a place, person or thing pertaining to the Celts," the teacher explained. "Remember, that brings you up to the Norman invasion of 1169."

"Must it be Celtic?" asked Gwendoline. "I don't know anything about the Celts."

Miss Ryan looked annoyed. "Really, Gwendoline," she remarked crossly, "even you can't be *that* ignorant. St Brigid's has an excellent library and I have arranged for all of you to visit the National Museum in Dublin and view the Celtic treasures there, in the hope that it might inspire you to great heights."

"When are we going to the museum?" asked an interested Fidelma. Miss Ryan smiled at her.

"I have ordered the coach for Wednesday week," she replied.

Judith, who had been studying her entry form, remarked, "The prizes are great, aren't they? I suppose we'll be entering the junior section."

"Yes," agreed the teacher. "And the first prize is a hundred pounds and a gold medal!"

"Oh, Miss Ryan," burst in Deirdre. "The President will be handing out the prizes—and on television too!"

"I thought that would impress you," observed the teacher. "Celtic Heritage Year is going to be a big thing with lots of events—pageants and plays and the like."

"That sounds brill. I'd love to see a pageant," cried Gráinne.

"Yes," agreed Miss Ryan enthusiastically. "Now, wouldn't it be marvellous if someone from St Brigid's won a prize! Think how proud your parents would be."

"My parents would die of shock if I won a history prize," commented Monica frankly.

Even Miss Ryan joined in the ripple of amusement which spread through the class. "Get out *Revolution and Recovery*," she ordered. "We've spent enough time on the entry forms; we'll come back to them again. Turn to page 126 and let's do a bit of work."

That evening, Aileen, whose anger had been simmering all day over Miss Ryan's remarks, voiced her feelings to the common room.

"You're quite right, Aileen," agreed Eithne. "I'm sick of teachers going on about Sr Gobnait and her ideas."

"Miss Ryan was horrible to you and I don't blame you if you feel like kicking her," chimed in Josie. There was a murmur of agreement from the other third-years. Aileen was mollified.

"We have to write the essay," pointed out Judith. "Wouldn't it be great if one of us did well, all the same. I'd love to have a hundred pounds to spend."

"We haven't a chance," said Nuala cheerfully. "But I mean to try. Think what it would do for the history club."

"I suppose if we have to write it anyway," agreed

Deirdre, "we might as well do the best we can, and of course it would be good for the school too."

Whatever Deirdre, Nuala and a few others might say about the essay competition, the majority of the class resented the imposition. Sr Gobnait hadn't been popular since the banning of *Together and Apart*, but now they saw her as Public Enemy Number 1, making school impossible for them.

This resentment came to a head a few days later, when Ciara and Gwendoline were late for breakfast one morning. They slipped unobtrusively into the refectory, only to be stopped by one of the special prefects. Irene O'Shea was detested by the third-years because of the very sarcastic and superior way she had of speaking to them. "That will be a pound each for the missions, thank you very much," she said jeeringly.

"Oh, Irene," pleaded Ciara. "A pound is an awful lot. Please give us a chance, please!"

Gwendoline wasn't worried about the pound but she knew Ciara hadn't much money, so she added her plea, "We were only a minute late, Irene."

"So little Miss Moneybags grudges a pound to the missions. For that, two pounds from you and one from Ciara. Next time, it will be detention as well," replied Irene, in a hard, nasty voice.

They were afraid to say any more so they just paid over the money, with rage in their hearts. That evening, a meeting was held in the common room involving Ciara, Gwendoline and six or seven others, victims of

Irene's particular nastiness. They vowed to get even with her as soon as the opportunity arose.

"We must think of something that can't be blamed on us," observed Ciara.

"Something really clever," agreed Gwendoline. "Now, everybody, think." Not surprisingly, none of them could think of anything clever and so the meeting was adjourned until further notice.

The days passed, and soon it was the sixth of February. The weather was unusually clement and the coach-load of girls arrived in the museum well before 2 p.m. Miss Ryan met them at the door and immediately led them off to the Celtic Treasures Room. Most of them had visited the museum before when they were in primary school, and weren't expecting much. To their surprise, Miss Ryan's talk and enthusiasm were infectious, and the time passed swiftly and enjoyably.

Aileen and Josie weren't very interested in history of any kind, and in consequence were first out the door when the lecture was over.

"What a brill day for February," declared Josie, as they stood waiting for the history teacher and the rest of the class to appear.

"Awesome," agreed Aileen enthusiastically. "Remember last year and all that snow."

A crowd of third-years came clattering down the steps of the museum, followed by Miss Ryan, who gathered the class around her. "Now, remember you must go in groups, no one on her own," she instructed them. "We'll meet at five o'clock. Be on time as we have to be back in school for tea. Is that clear?"

There was a chorus of "Yes, Miss Ryan." Then the girls moved away from the museum and down the street, dividing up into small groups as they did so. When they got to Dawson Street, Nuala and company discussed what they wanted to do next.

"Let's go to McDonald's," urged Aileen. "There must be something wrong with me, but a couple of hours looking at Celtic treasures has made me hungry."

"Me too," agreed Eithne. "It's not that I don't admire the Tara Brooch or the Ardagh Chalice and all the rest but I feel the need for nourishment after all that history." She looked enquiringly at her twin, who said she felt the very same.

"You're a couple of philistines," corrected Nuala severely. "Who else is for burger and chips?"

"I have to buy a present for my little sister's birthday next week," Josie mentioned. "I thought I would try Switzer's: they have lots of toys there."

"Righto," agreed Nuala. "I'll go with you. What about you, Judith?"

"I don't mind. I don't feel very hungry so I'll go with you. We can all meet later at the top of the street." They split up into two groups, promising to meet again at the coach.

It didn't take long to get to Switzer's basement and soon Judith, Nuala and Josie were enjoying themselves looking at the toys there. Eventually, Josie decided to buy a little family of green frogs, dressed in pretty cotton dresses and shirts, for her sister's birthday present.

As they were leaving the shop, Josie, who was a little ahead of the other two, suddenly turned and plucked at Nuala's sleeve. "Look," she cried, pointing at something across the street. "There's the woman who was in the National Gallery—the one with the wrong face, I mean."

Nuala looked in the direction Josie was pointing, but at first all she could see were the shifting crowds of people walking up and down Grafton Street. Then she noticed, through a sudden gap in the crowd, a woman standing on the opposite side of the street, looking thunderous.

She drew Josie nervously back into the shop and said, "I'm not surprised she looked familiar to you. If it weren't for the thick black curls, I'd say you'd have recognised her at once as someone you know very well."

She whispered something to a mystified Judith, who gave a startled yip and peeped out through the glass door of the shop. "You're right, Nuala," she confirmed in a shocked whisper. "It's the person who ran around St Brigid's last year calling herself Sr Mercy."

Josie pushed Judith aside impatiently and took a long look across the street. "I never saw her in ordinary clothes before," she said at last. "But now that you mention it, I remember that bad-tempered expression. I wonder who's the lucky guy she's waiting for."

"Well, I suppose we should go on our way,"

suggested Nuala. "She can't do much to us now."

"You're right," agreed Judith. "If anything, it's the other way around."

So the three girls walked out the main door of Switzer's, just in time to see a tall, well-dressed man join the woman on the other side of the street. They gathered from the gestures he was making that he was apologising for keeping her waiting. As they watched, he threw an arm affectionately around the woman's shoulder and then the two of them went off together towards Trinity College.

Judith was startled by Nuala, who let out a deep breath and gasped, "Whew, what a merry-go-round. That man was Dr Waldron from St Winifred's Clinic!"

"What's so special about that?" cried Josie in surprise.

"Nothing, maybe, but the last time I saw him, Nurse Beatty was hanging out of his arm. I was sure they were an item."

"Oh, look at the time," cried Josie. "It's nearly five. We'd better hurry."

As they hurried up Grafton Street, Nuala said breathlessly: "Don't say anything to the others until we're back. We'll have a meeting about it tonight."

Judith nodded her head in agreement.

"I wish you'd write and tell Bill. He said to get in touch with him if anything peculiar turned up," Josie reminded them.

"Maybe, but we'll have the meeting anyway,"

Nuala insisted.

The third-years' arrival back at the the school coincided with that of the jubilant First eleven. They had won their match and were now in the semi-finals of the Boyne Cup. "Isn't it marvellous? I never thought we'd make it," confessed Josie, when they were all in the cloakroom changing for tea.

"I'm not really surprised," came Gwendoline's voice from behind her. "During the Christmas holidays, Sr Gobnait met Miss Keane in Rome and she probably picked up a few tips from her and that's how they won."

"What a lucky break for St Brigid's," was Josie's comment, a sentiment with which everyone agreed.

As they were all leaving the refectory after tea that evening, Ciara drew Gwendoline aside. "I've a great idea to get even with Irene," she whispered. "Will you give me a hand?"

Gwendoline nodded excitedly. "You bet," she whispered back. "What's the plan?"

Ciara held up a white plastic box. "Here's the secret weapon. Come on. I'll tell you about it as we go along."

That night, as most of the school were drifting up to bed talking and laughing, the air was rent by hideous screams coming from the sixth-year bedrooms. Sr Gobnait, who seemed to be always hanging around the dormitories, at once rushed off in the direction of the screaming.

She went straight to one of the rooms and flung

open the door, revealing a white-faced, sobbing Irene. "What's the matter?" asked the concerned nun.

Irene, trembling, threw back the quilt on her bed, revealing two enormous spiders, black against the white sheets.

Sr Gobnait picked them up and walked over to the window. When she had deposited them outside, she closed the window firmly. Then she gave the badly shaken prefect a brisk lecture on keeping her nerve and on showing the younger girls good example.

Quite a crowd had gathered around the open door by this time. They listened with appreciation to the Major, boring on about cowardice and bad example to Irene O'Shea, one of her nasty special prefects.

Gwendoline and Ciara went back to their dormitories, laughing and giggling all the way. When Gwendoline parted from Ciara, she hurried to tell Nuala all about it. Nuala, who was already in bed, paid scant attention to her. She was fully occupied in writing a letter to Bill Crilly. The rest of the gang had decided that this was the best course of action.

A few days later, Bill Crilly drove over to Nurse Beatty's flat. There were a few questions he wanted to ask her. He stayed there for quite a long time.

15

Tara at St Brigid's!

"Nuala! Is Nuala here?" called Judith, coming into the common room and waving a letter in the air.

"What do you want Nuala for?" asked Monica eagerly.

"Oh, just something..." Judith replied in a vague way.

"She's at the back of the room with Aileen and Josie," replied a disappointed Monica, pointing to where Nuala and company were absorbed in a keen game of Monopoly.

"Hi, Nuala," Judith called as she reached the table.

"Hi, chuck," replied Nuala absently, her mind on the game. "What's the crack?"

"Well, the funniest thing has happened. I had a letter from home and apparently a cousin of Dad's turned up last week out of the blue. He hadn't seen her since they were kids. What's more, she took a fancy to that painting I did of St Brigid's as a Christmas present, and Mum wants me to paint one for Kate; that's the cousin's name!"

"Why don't you just give her one of the other ones you painted?" suggested Eithne. "They were very good, too."

"I had forgotten all about them," Judith said joyfully. "I wonder what happened to them."

Nuala passed a card to Aileen. "Forty pounds, please, Aileen," and without looking up she answered, "Mrs McGlade put them away in the art room. Don't you remember, Judith?"

"Did she? Thanks, Nuala, I'll go there and root them out," said Judith, leaving them to continue their game in peace.

A short while later she returned, carrying one rolled-up canvas. "I searched high and low in that wretched room," she complained. "And all I could find was this one. There wasn't a sign of the other."

"You'll have to ask Ma McGlade about it on Friday," Nuala cheerfully said.

Before Judith could answer, the door burst open and Gwendoline almost fell into the room, shouting, "Hurray! Hurray! Tara is coming to St Brigid's to do a *Jungle* ad: I think this Thursday!"

All the year crowded around her, some asking questions, others merely cheering excitedly. "You're not having us on, are you?" asked Aileen, with painful intensity, when the excitement had died down a bit.

Gwendoline repudiated the suggestion

indignantly. "Of course not. Mummy rang up a few minutes ago with the great news!"

"What time on Thursday?" asked Gráinne. "Will we be at class?"

"Mummy says that it's supposed to be about eleven in the morning but she thought that the television cameras and things would be here much earlier."

"I wonder how they persuaded Sr Gobnait," mused Josie. "I thought she hated *Jungle*."

"They had quite a job to get her to agree, I believe, but she gave in eventually. I suppose the money they gave towards the swimming-pool helped," observed Gwendoline shrewdly.

"We have science on Thursday at that time," said Deirdre. "We won't even be near the castle then."

"What about the little stockroom above the lab?" asked Aileen. "I could pretend I needed test-tubes or something, go up and take a quick look out. If there's anything going on, I will come down and pass the word along."

"Good idea," said Gráinne. "We could take it in turns to go up and watch."

"Miss Crilly hasn't red hair for nothing," warned Nuala. "We can't *all* be needing new test-tubes or books."

"I think it's a waste of time anyway," observed Eithne. "You'd see nothing up there. We'll just have to rush out of class early and hope that she's still in the school."

"I'm sure Sr Gobnait picked Thursday because she knew we would be out of the way then," said Gwendoline, sounding quite vicious. Everyone agreed with her, thinking how typical it was of the Major to prevent the third-years from getting a little pleasure in their dull, hard lives.

Thursday morning found them straggling reluctantly across to the lab after break. There wasn't any sign of television cameras or crew and the girls began to think that Mrs O'Hagan had got the day wrong.

Half way through class, Miss Crilly, running short of chalk, by a happy chance picked on Aileen to run upstairs and get some more from the stockroom. It was the work of a moment to get the chalk. Aileen was about to go down again when something made her look out the window.

The science lab originally had been the castle stables, which were situated a little distance from the castle itself. On three sides it faced into the yard, but on the fourth side it overlooked a pretty little garden situated about fifty yards away. Aileen's eyes widened as she saw a procession of people coming in through the gate of this garden, led by Sr Gobnait. Two other nuns, and two women unknown to Aileen, followed the Major. Then came two men carrying cameras. In the middle of the group, she could see what was obviously a person of some importance, tenderly escorting Tara. She wore the school uniform and her long fair hair glinted in the sun.

Forcing herself to walk calmly down the stairs, Aileen handed the chalk over to Miss Crilly and went back to her place. She sat down and tore a page from her copy. She wrote furiously on this and then passed it to Josie, who read it excitedly and passed it to Eithne. It didn't take long for the news to circulate around the room, causing ripples of uneasy whispering among the girls.

Miss Crilly looked sharply at them, but before she could make any comment the door opened and Sr Imelda came in. All apologies for disturbing her at class, but she wanted to have urgent speech with her. She drew Miss Crilly aside and to everyone's delight, both teachers walked over to the door and passed through it, talking animatedly.

As soon as the door closed behind them, Aileen, followed by the whole class, made a dash for the stockroom, taking the stairs two steps at a time. Within minutes they were crowding around the windows, hoping to catch a glimpse of their favourite television star.

Silence fell on the third-years as they noticed Tara sitting on a bench beside the sundial with a guitar. As she sat there, one of the women came over and dusted her face with something and, as she walked away, another woman brushed the already perfect hair. Then the cameramen took up their positions.

Aileen, anxious not to miss a magic moment,

opened the window and scrambled out on the sill. Then she stretched up and pulled herself onto the flat roof, which was just above the window. Settling herself comfortably, she watched admiringly as Tara took up the guitar and started to accompany herself, singing some catchy tune. At her feet lay a large cat, which Aileen recognised with a thrill as Wrinkles the lion.

Meanwhile outside the lab door, Miss Crilly said goodbye to Sr Imelda and returned to her classroom, only to find it deserted. Hearing a lot of noise coming from the stockroom, the puzzled teacher mounted the stairs, looking her grimmest.

However, when she saw her excited pupils all crowded around the windows, curiosity won the day. Pushing her way through the girls, she looked down on the scene below. To everyone's amazement, she exclaimed, "What beautiful long hair; I didn't think hair like that existed nowadays. Who is she, and look at that enormous cat! Who are they?"

With one voice the third-years answered: "Tara, the Teenage Terror and Wrinkles her lion cub!"

Miss Crilly laughed. "I see," she replied. "Come along now; back to the lab. We've wasted enough class time already."

As the girls left the room, she closed and locked the windows before following them downstairs. It was some time before Nuala and Judith realised that Aileen hadn't returned with them. Then Nuala remembered seeing her climbing out the window. They had to wait an agonising fifteen minutes before the bell went for the end of class.

Without waiting for permission, Nuala, closely followed by Judith, ran out of the lab into the yard, wondering how they would get Aileen down from the roof.

They were halted by the sight of two men holding a long ladder which was propped against the building. As they watched, a flustered and excited Aileen stepped off the last rung of the ladder and grasped the outstretched hand of her heroine, Tara, who was standing waiting for her.

Nuala and Judith went over to join Aileen, who called excitedly to them, "Tara rescued me from the roof. Isn't she brill!"

"It was nothing," said Tara modestly. "I just told the tall nun and she got the men and the ladder."

Nuala and Judith looked in admiration at the girl who could tell Sr Gobnait what to do and get away with it.

The rest of the third-years came rushing over and soon Tara was surrounded by devoted fans, shouting excitedly and asking her questions. "Why are you here, Tara?" asked Gráinne. "Is it another advertisement?"

"Not really," Tara smiled back. "They are thinking of starring me in a serial for children's television about an adventure in a boarding school and we are trying out a few schools, to see which one would be the best for the purpose."

"Oh, I hope it's here," breathed Aileen, all starry-eyed. "They might even let us be extras!" There was a loud murmur of excited agreement from the other girls.

"Where's Wrinkles?" asked Josie.

"Wrinkles has gone home," replied Tara. "He causes such a lot of excitement when I take him around. Crowds excite him a bit; he is very young, you know."

"Girls, what are you doing here?" The stern voice of Sr Gobnait broke across the chatter. "Go to dinner at once. Tara, dear, come with me and I will take you back to your mother."

"Yes, sister. Goodbye, everybody," called Tara, and she went off with Sr Gobnait.

"Goodbye, Tara. Come again soon," called back the third-years.

Her clear voice carried back to them. "This is a fab place. I would like to make the series in St Brigid's."

Naturally, the third-years could talk of nothing else all that evening or for the next few days. Friday afternoon, as usual, was given over to art and Mrs McGlade found the girls very restless and giddy throughout the hour and forty minutes of class. As time went on she got crosser and crosser. Judith, suddenly remembering her lost canvas, went up to the teacher just before the end of class. "Please, Mrs McGlade," she began politely.

"Well, what is it?" snapped the teacher.

Judith was surprised; she had never heard that note in her voice before. "I just wanted to ask you about a lost canvas of mine. I did three last term. They were different views of the school and river. You may remember that I gave one to Mum and Dad for Christmas and you took the other two back to this room."

Before she could say another thing about the lost pictures, Mrs McGlade looked at her with glittering eyes and cut her short with a hiss. "Are you accusing me of stealing your canvas? Do you think that I go around taking pupils' work?"

"Oh, no!" gasped a horrified Judith. "I wouldn't dream of such a thing. It's just I can't find the third one and I thought you might, might..." and her voice trailed away as she saw the look on the teacher's face.

"I just scuttled back to my place," she told Nuala later. "I just can't believe Mrs McGlade could look like that. I was absolutely terrified of her!"

"I am surprised," agreed Nuala. "She is usually so quiet, almost mouselike. Then you're supposed to be quite a pet of hers, aren't you?"

"I don't know about that," replied a rueful Judith, "but it's funny all the same. Why did she think that I thought she stole them?"

"There's something else," Nuala pointed out. "I wonder what *did* happen to your picture."

"I don't know. I can't see what anyone would want it for!" exclaimed Judith.

16

Junior A Wins Through

At about the same time as Tara was singing in the garden of St Brigid's, Bill Crilly parked his car outside a neat bungalow on the Trim road, got out and walked up the short drive. He had hardly pressed the bell when the door opened and a tall, pleasant young woman stood in front of him. "Can I help you?" she enquired with a slight smile.

Bill smiled back. "Yes, please. I am looking for Miss Julia O'Keeffe who acts as relief night matron at St Winifreds's Clinic."

The woman looked startled. "I am Julia O'Keeffe—well, at least, I was. Should I know you?" she enquired.

"I am acting for an insurance company, investigating a small fire in St Winifreds's last October," he answered smoothly. "I believe you were on night duty then."

She shook her head and eyed him curiously. "No, I wasn't. I haven't worked in St Winifred's for a year at least. My husband doesn't like me doing night work," she explained.

"Oh, I am so sorry. The clinic must have mixed you up with someone else. I apologise for bothering you." Bill smiled again and walked back to his car.

"That's all right," she replied, watching him get into the car and drive away.

"I wonder what he really wanted," she muttered to herself, as she went back into her sitting-room. "I suppose I'll never know. Maybe I was foolish to let Josephine do my night duty in the clinic last October. She's a funny sort, but very generous with the money." And she looked fondly at an expensive couch and two armchairs, obviously purchased quite recently.

"Well, was she the right one?" asked Bill of his passenger, as he drove away from the bungalow.

"No, she wasn't," answered a surprised Anne Beatty. "I don't know who she is—a complete stranger in fact."

"That's not surprising, since she says she hasn't worked in St Winifred's for a year at least. Her husband objects to her doing night duty."

"The plot thickens," laughed Anne.

"You're right," he grinned. "Could we go to your flat? There is something I want to ask you and it will be more private there."

She looked warily at him but all she said was, "That's fine with me. Take the first turn left."

Some time later as they sat drinking coffee in her tiny kitchen, Bill, who had been silent for a while, asked,

"Will you level with me, Anne? It's important."

Anne put down her mug. "Yes, on one condition: I must ask you a question first." He nodded and she went on, "Are you a private detective?"

Bill laughed. "I can't blame you for asking that. As it happens, I am a historian, not a PI, but I do seem to keep getting mixed up in mysteries. Now my question: are you seriously involved with Kenneth Waldron?"

She hesitated for a moment and answered, "I know him, of course, but there is nothing between us. I don't believe he is interested in me either, even though he puts up a show of affection even in public."

"That's good, because I have good reason to believe that he is two-timing you with someone in Dublin," Bill said grimly.

"I see I will have to tell you my story," Anne replied. "Then I hope you will tell me yours. Several years ago, Ken Waldron was partially responsible for the death of a dear friend of mine. She had loved him and he had framed her in a drugs case in England. Before she died, she told me all about it. Anyway, as things fell out, our paths crossed in St Winifred's Clinic. He pretended that he was interested in me, I don't know why, but I suspect he was up to something illegal there with the night matron. I don't know what it is; sometimes I suspect blackmail! All I know is that the two of them were up to no good. I thought that if I pretended to like him too, I could find out what it was. I can't say I've had much success," she ended glumly.

Bill looked sympathetically at her. "I see I'll have to tell you my side now." He smiled at her and plunged into the whole story of the events in St Brigid's the previous year and what Nuala and Judith had told him this year.

"So you think that Ken and these women are involved in collecting stuff from a hidden passageway in the school? It sounds fantastic," she cried. "Is it buried treasure, do you think?"

"I don't know what to think, but something is going on, and the school and the clinic seem to be connected," he answered. "Will you give us a hand at your end?"

"Certainly, but I don't think I am much use at this kind of thing. Still, I'll pass on anything I find out," she promised.

"That's great," replied Bill. "It also gives me a good excuse to take you out quite often."

She raised her coffee cup. "I'll drink to that," she said, smiling.

A few days later Josie came into the common room, announcing that the Junior Boyne Cup match was fixed for the following Wednesday.

"It's very early this year, isn't it?" Monica observed.

"That's because Easter's early this year," answered Josie. "Have you forgotten that we break up on Tuesday 27 March?"

"What a beautiful thought," murmured Judith.

"I suppose the senior match will be the following week," said Gráinne.

"It will be the first year that we have both teams in the cup—not that we have a chance with either of them," added Aileen gloomily.

Nuala finished reading her book and closed it. She got up and walked over to Josie, saying, "I have a great idea. Look at Josie. We know that she has potential; so I'll take her under my wing and we'll all help her to prepare for the match."

"What exactly do you mean?" asked Josie nervously.

Nuala walked around her. "Let me see: you've bags under your eyes. Gráinne and Deirdre, make sure that she gets to sleep early every night even if you have to knock her out!"

"Hey, Nuala, cut it out," protested Josie. "I am perfectly fit. I don't need your help."

Nuala shook her head in mock reproof. "Now, now, Josie, you eat far too many sweets. Twins, sit beside her for the next week. Can I depend on you? Don't let her eat fatty foods, too much sugar—you know that kind of thing."

"We'll do it. It'll be a pleasure," replied the twins, grinning at Josie.

"Judith and Aileen, supervise her jogging every morning. You see, Josie, you are the only third-year on the team and we want you to snatch victory for the school. With our help, you might even score the winning goal!"

"It's a great idea, Nuala!" said Aileen. "We will all take it in turn to coach her. Sr Gobnait is concentrating on the first eleven, so she won't have any time for Junior A."

Josie, who had thought that it was only one of Nuala's jokes, found to her disgust that the whole of third year took their new responsibilities very seriously.

Nuala drew up a rota and every day except for class times, Josie was accompanied by two girls, who supervised her eating, sleeping and exercise training.

Wednesday arrived at last, to Josie's relief. After an early dinner, the whole school repaired to the hockey pitch, as it was a home match. Third-years ranged themselves at strategic points around the pitch, prepared to cheer Junior A to victory.

In the "Teams Only" room, Nuala formally pinned a little silver lion mascot on Josie's Aertex shirt. "This has been presented by all the year to show our support—and affection, of course," she pronounced solemnly. "I have arranged groups around the pitch, so anywhere the play goes, you will have somebody cheering you on. You look terrific and fit. Go out now and win!"

Josie gave her a hunted look and answered, "It will be a miracle if I play well, after all the persecution you've inflicted on me for the past week."

"I don't grudge one bit of all the trouble I went to to get you in good shape for the match," replied Nuala, in all sincerity. She hadn't done much really, except to direct the more than willing third-years in their duties.

Neither side scored until half way through the second half, when St Catherine's gained the lead with one goal, quickly equalised by St Brigid's. Excitement reached fever pitch as each side moved up and down the field. Just five minutes before the referee was due to blow the whistle, Josie was passed the ball. She flew down the pitch, miraculously avoiding the St Catherine's backs, took a desperate chance and shot the winning goal.

The hoarse third-years made a supreme effort and cheered her again and again. A delighted Sr Gobnait congratulated her warmly with a whole series of "Simply splendids."

She was escorted triumphantly back to the castle by her year, who were convinced that the victory was due entirely to their efforts.

Judith was called to the phone after tea, while the remainder of the gang went on up to the common room. They had study off that night in celebration of winning the cup. There was talk of a video in the gym instead.

Nuala, remembering that she had left her watch in the cloakroom, went down to collect it. As she was leaving the cloakroom, she met an excited Judith who dragged her up to the dormitory to hear all about her phone call. Perching herself on her bed, she motioned Nuala to the chair. "Nuala, do you remember all that fuss in the papers last year about some millionaire called McMahon? Remember, he died in America and left three paintings by Picasso to the National Gallery."

"I do, vaguely," answered Nuala. "Aren't they having a grand opening or unveiling some time, full of VIPs and all that sort of jazz!"

Judith, flushed with excitement, nodded in agreement. "That's the very one, that's what my phone call was about. Mum and Dad have been invited to the grand opening."

Nuala was impressed. "I never knew that your parents were VIPs."

Judith laughed. "They aren't: it's all Dr Beverly-Morrissey," she said.

"Come again? This doctor with the double-barrelled name is a relation of yours?"

"No, but he is married to Kate, Dad's cousin—the long-lost one! I sent a painting of St Brigid's to her, remember? Anyway he is doing the unveiling on the big night, and Kate has invited not only my parents but me too—and a friend!"

"That's brilliant!" replied Nuala warmly. "You'll really enjoy that. I suppose you'll take one of the twins."

"Mum has invited *you*, Nuala. She wants you to ring your mother and find out if she'll let you go. You see: it's on the twenty-sixth, the day before we break up. They'll be flying over on the Monday morning and you can stay with us in Dublin. We'll have a bit of fun there."

"It's marvellous of you," stammered Nuala. "I

really don't know what to say."

Judith pushed her out the door of the dormitory. "Don't say anything, just go down and ring home and get permission. I'll do the rest."

17

Gallery Goings-On

The Easter exams started on 18 March and in keeping with Sr Gobnait's policy the teachers had outdone one another in setting sneaky papers. Many were the complaints from third-years who hadn't bothered to study hard.

On Wednesday the twenty-first, Nuala, desperate to get some study done, went up to the dormitory after a quick breakfast. She wasn't there long when Judith arrived, asking, "What are you doing here? I've been looking for you everywhere."

Nuala groaned. "I wanted to go over a few things for the Irish exam this afternoon. Did you want me for anything special?"

"Yes, the post came," replied Judith, throwing two letters on Nuala's bed.

"Thanks," said Nuala, picking them up and slitting them open. "This one's from home...Brill! Mum has to go to Dublin on Monday and she'll pick us up here and bring us to the airport in time to meet your parents."

"That's marvellous. I can look forward to Monday now. I was dreading the bus; it always make me feel sick."

"Poor Ju. I can send my luggage home with her too. This letter's from Bill Crilly. He says that in pursuit of the mysterious night matron, he and Nurse Beatty are going to Dublin until Tuesday or Wednesday. He gives us his phone number in Dublin and says to ring him if anything at all turns up."

"It looks as if he is getting desperate, doesn't it?" commented Judith, picking up the letter and reading it. "I don't believe they'll ever find her." There was no answer from Nuala, who was studying again. Judith walked over to the window and looked out. She watched Sr Gobnait running up and down the towpath, shouting orders to the two teams straining at the oars, as they rowed on the river.

"She's right to get them back on the river. It will help them to forget their terrible defeat in the Boyne Cup," she commented.

Nuala shook her head, and replied more in sorrow than in anger, "If only she had asked *my* advice, the Boyne Cup would be standing proudly amongst all the others in the gym now!"

Judith had to laugh, but hastened to agree loyally. "I'm sure you're right; you did wonders for Josie!"

Nuala sighed and said: "What else can you expect from a woman who steps out of holes in walls and frightens poor third-years!"

Judith shuddered. "Don't remind me of that day," she begged. "Now that you mention it, she hasn't stepped out of the wall once this whole term."

"We frightened her good and proper," Nuala replied complacently. "She's afraid to use that corridor while we are here. I'd love to know why she did it. Wouldn't you?"

"I would; after all there's no reason for her not to do it openly. It's *her* castle, after all," replied Judith.

"Mmm, you've a point there. Did you hear that she got a present of several cases of *Jungle* from the manufacturers!"

"Yes, and Aileen is in ecstasies over a letter from Tara. She was reading it to the whole year as I came up here. It's nearly half-nine. We'd better rush." Nuala gathered up her books. "It's history, isn't it? I hope Miss Ryan's kinder in her questions than the others were."

Judith handed Bill Crilly's letter to her. "Put it away in a safe place. We may need that phone number yet." Nuala carefully tucked it into her purse. They left the dormitory and hurried down to join the rest of the class.

The last exam, which took place on Friday the twenty-third, was art. When it was over, Mrs McGlade collected their paintings and called for silence. "There's one thing I have to say to you," she began. "I have arranged with Sr Gobnait for the whole school to watch the special television coverage of the presentation of the

McMahon legacy to the nation on Monday afternoon. He bequeathed three major works of art by Picasso!"

Eithne broke in. "Judith and Nuala are going to the presentation and the reception afterwards."

"Judith's father is a cousin of Mrs Beverly-Morrissey," Fidelma proudly informed the teacher.

Mrs McGlade beamed at Judith, who was quite embarrassed by all this attention. "How wonderful!" she cried. "You lucky pair! You'll probably see me there too. The rest of you needn't be jealous, though. The presentation is scheduled to start at 3 p.m. but Sr Gobnait has promised to arrange the timetable on Tuesday so that you can watch from 1.30 p.m., when the cameras will take you on a tour of the gallery. The commentary will be by a famous artist, and it will teach you a lot about the great works of art there. I am sure you'll all love it."

"You won't be here, then?" asked Monica, deciding not to bother watching the tour of the gallery.

"No, dear," replied Mrs McGlade, who seemed to be in very good humour. "I start my holidays today. As your art teacher, I can't emphasise enough how important it is that you should watch the whole programme on Monday, though." And she looked sternly at Monica, who coloured guiltily.

Later on quite a crowd stood outside the castle and waved goodbye to Miss Ryan and Mrs McGlade as they whizzed off down the avenue in the latter's white car. Judith commented to Nuala, "They made a great thing of saying goodbye, didn't they? The Easter holidays are two weeks long. You'd think they were leaving the school for ever."

"I don't remember teachers making such a fuss before," agreed Nuala. "Miss Ryan is all right, though. I was talking to her about the history competition and she was very helpful. She says that the minute we get back, she will start us off. She's really keen for someone to get a prize."

They turned and went into the castle. Aileen joined them as they approached the common room. "Sr Gobnait has just put a notice on the board inviting all the third-years to a *Jungle* party on Saturday!" she announced happily to them.

"Tara had a great effect on her, hadn't she?"

"Three cheers for Tara," called Judith, thinking about the nun's earlier views on *Jungle*.

"I don't believe it but it's been proved true," cried Nuala, throwing open the common room door. She flung out one arm dramatically and announced to the girls in there: "Ads do tell the truth after all: *Jungle* has tamed Gobnait the Ghostly!"

18

Goodbye, Gallery

Bill felt his spirits rise as he walked through St Stephen's Green on his way back from Mass on the following Sunday. The sunlight falling on beds of daffodils and crocuses, particularly rich after the mild winter, helped him to forget the disappointments of the last week. For, despite all his efforts—and he had tried hard—he couldn't find a trace of the mysterious night matron of St Winifred's. He decided to ring Anne Beatty, who was staying with a friend in Donnybrook. When she answered the phone, his first question was, "Any news of Dr Waldron?"

Anne's voice came thinly over the line. "Not a thing. I must have rung twenty times. There was no answer; maybe they've both left the country."

"Maybe. Let's forget them for the present. Would you care to be dined and wined?" he asked.

"I'd love it. What time will you call?"

"About 6.30. We'll go into Frederico's and make an

evening of it."

He put down the phone and went off whistling cheerfully to check the car. That evening, as they drove down an almost empty Merrion Street, a white van shot past them. Bill watched it as it speedily passed through Merrion Square and turned the corner into Clare Street.

"Someone seems in a great hurry," he said to Anne, who smiled back at him. Immediately the white van slipped from his mind, which was a pity, as half way down Clare Street it turned to the right and went down a lane, which led into another one and eventually a cul-de-sac. There the driver backed the van through the open doors of a garage. Immediately, a dark-haired woman dressed in black came forward and closed the garage doors.

The driver jumped down, taking off dark glasses. "Hi, countess!" he called cheerfully, showing his white teeth. "Everything under control?"

"Need you ask, Ken? Where's Jo?"

"I'm here in the back," said a quiet voice. "Come on you two, give a hand."

Ken and the countess immediately went to the back of the van, where Jo handed down three large parcels, neatly packaged in brown paper.

Then the countess led the way out of a side door in the garage, followed by the others. They each carried a brown parcel. She locked the door behind them.

They passed swiftly though various passages and back yards until they reached a wall. The man helped the women to climb over the wall; then he passed the parcels over to them and scrambled over it himself.

It was dark on the other side of the wall. They could just discern the outlines of a large building ahead of them.

"That's the art gallery," whispered the countess. "The back door is just over here." Switching on a small torch, she led them across a paved surface. When she stopped, they could see in the dim light cast by the torch that they were standing in front of a wooden door set in a wall of the dark, massive building.

As soon as the countess knocked on this door, it flew open. A woman stood there. She spoke with a nervous inflection to her voice. "What kept the pair of you?"

"Sorry Pat," said Ken. "We couldn't help it." He took a bunch of keys out of his pocket and held them out to Pat. "Are these yours?" he asked. "I found them in my car."

She glanced indifferently at them. "Not mine," she replied. "The countess. I'll give them to her." Ken followed the other two women, who were nearly out of sight by now. Pat locked the door and hurried after him.

It had got quite dark but the countess led the way through the building without hesitation. The only time she used her torch was when they reached the door of the Long Room and she had to pick out a key. Once again the silence was broken by the one called Pat. "Are you sure there are no special beams or anything like that in there?" her voice was jumpy as she asked.

"That's all been attended to," replied the countess calmly. She went straight over to the curtains and looped them back.

Ken took down the paintings hanging there and passed them to the countess. At the same time, Jo and Pat carefully removed the brown paper from the parcels, revealing three other pictures. Ken hung these up with the help of the countess, while the other two carefully wrapped the Picassos in the discarded brown paper.

The countess dropped the curtain back into place. As she did so, she flashed her torch for a second on the last painting. "Excellent copy, Pat!" she said in a satisfied voice.

The countess checked that the room was perfectly in order. Then she pushed the others out the door and locked it again.

Jo and Pat left, each carrying a picture, and as Ken picked up his, he whispered: "Meet me at Jury's tomorrow at noon. We can have a celebration lunch."

The countess whispered back, "See you tomorrow then, *cara*." She closed the door behind him and bolted it.

When she had done some necessary little jobs in the security room, she went downstairs to the basement. Locking herself into the cleaners' room there, she set an alarm clock for eight a.m. Then she lay down on some rugs and was soon fast asleep on her improvised bed.

When the rest of the cleaners turned up for work

next morning, they were edified to see the countess already at work, dressed in a blue overall and curly black wig and singing tunefully as she washed one of the marble floors.

As soon as Ken reached the garage he put his dark glasses on again. Then he drove the white van out into the cul-de-sac. The garage doors were closed by Pat, who climbed into the seat beside the driver, saying, "Drop me off at Stephen's Green."

Some time later, when the van pulled up to the rear of a block of flats in Ballsbridge, Ken found that Jo had already cut the canvases from their frames and placed them in a special case, which she had brought for that purpose.

She got out of the van and faced him on the pavement. "Coming in for a drink?" she asked him, yawning.

"No, I don't think so. I have to get rid of the frames and van. See you tomorrow," he replied. She watched the van drive away. Then she went into her flat and placed the case in a wall safe, which she locked carefully. Feeling tired after a hard evening's work, she too retired to bed and slept soundly until morning.

19

Double Dealings

Nuala was swiftly stripping her bed on Monday morning when Aileen came in to the dormitory. "Hi, Nuala. Are you packed yet?" she asked as she perched herself on a window seat. "What time is your mother collecting you?"

Nuala briskly shoved sheets and pillowcases into her laundry bag. "Hi, chuck! About eleven-thirty. I hope the fog will have lifted by then. Judith is worried about her parents' plane getting safely to Dublin Airport," she added anxiously.

Aileen looked out the window. "It's not that bad; I can see the sun shining through it. I wish I were going home today."

"Really, Aileen! You'll be going tomorrow. That reminds me: whatever happens, the four of you must watch the Major, today and tomorrow, like hawks!"

Aileen was puzzled. "What ever for? What's the Major done?" she asked plaintively.

"Surely you can't have forgotten it's the end of term and that's when we caught her before, getting out of the wall in the dormitory corridor!" Nuala replied in amazement.

"Well, I think it's crazy. Why should she do it again today? But I'll tell the others. It might help to pass the time."

Nuala looked frowningly at her. "I don't like your attitude at all. It looks as if you don't take this hole in the wall seriously. I wish we weren't going to this art thing now!"

"We'd better go," answered Aileen hastily. "It's almost nine and Sr Imelda sent me to tell everyone to be early for class, as we are having an extra-early dinner today."

Nuala cheered up. "That's so you can watch Judith and myself mixing with all the VIPs," she laughed. She picked up her luggage and followed Aileen out of the room.

The O'Briens' plane was due to touch down in Dublin at midday. However, when Judith, Nuala and her mother arrived at the airport, they were informed that all flights in and out had been delayed by the fog, which was now dispersing at last.

"Let's go up and have something to eat," suggested Mrs O'Donnell, looking at Judith's disappointed face. "I am sure you two are starving and I could do with a cup of coffee at least."

"Good idea," agreed Nuala. "It seems years since

breakfast. What about you, Ju?"

"Yes, please," replied Judith politely.

As they were going up on the escalator to the restaurant, Nuala had the feeling that the man ahead of them bore a strong resemblance to Dr Waldron. She didn't mention it to the others, though, as she wasn't really sure. When they arrived at the restaurant, she forgot about him, as she helped Judith to pick out something suitable for them to eat. Mrs O'Donnell contented herself with coffee and a biscuit.

They had finished their meal and were about to leave when it was announced over the loudspeakers: "Would Dr Kenneth Waldron, passenger for flight EI 706 to New York, please come at once to reception."

She heard Judith gasp and say: "He must be leaving the country. I wonder if Bill met him in Dublin after all."

Nuala thought for a moment and then hunted frantically for her purse. She held up a piece of folded paper and left the table saying, "I'll be back in a moment, Mum. I've got to make a phone call!"

Judith, resisting the impulse to follow her, sat down and said, "I think I should fill you in on why Nuala has rushed off to phone Bill."

The phone rang and rang and Nuala began to fear that Bill wasn't there. She was about to hang up when the ringing stopped and she recognised Bill's voice saying "Hello." Sighing with relief, she told him what she had seen and heard in the restaurant.

"We've been trying to get him all week," Bill said.

"I'll go straight out to the airport. I hope I'll be in time to see him before the plane leaves. Thanks, Nuala. See you later," he said as he put down the phone.

It must have been thirty-five minutes later that an anxious Nuala and Judith saw Bill's familiar figure striding through the reception area, almost five minutes after passengers for flight EI706 had been told to assemble at gate 14.

Nuala ran over and clutched Bill's sleeve. "You're too late," she said. "They've gone through to the boarding area."

Bill smiled ruefully at her. "I know, I know. Don't blame me. As soon as I had finished talking to you, Anne Beatty rang me. She has been trying for days to contact Ken Waldron. She thought she would try just once more this morning and by some miracle he answered the phone as he was about to leave for the airport. At first he denied knowing anything about night matron O'Keeffe, except that he thought that she was interested only in nursing—"

"Like the way she was interested in education last year, I suppose!" Nuala broke in.

Bill laughed. "Anyway, Anne then told him she knew O'Keeffe was really Jo O'Leary and that she had evidence that the two of them were doing something illegal in St Winifred's. At that he begged her not to expose him. He claimed that he was an innocent victim of Jo O'Leary and that he was leaving for the States today in an effort to get away from her. As proof of his good faith he revealed that Jo O'Leary and the countess had some contact in St Brigid's and that all three of them would be down there today carrying out some nefarious scheme or other. He didn't know any more than that. I don't believe a word of it but I think I should investigate it, all the same, especially in view of this secret passage business."

"He could have made the whole thing up," mused Nuala. "On the other hand there *is* something funny going on in St B's."

Judith and Mrs O'Donnell had joined them by now. "What's the latest? Did you catch Dr Waldron?" asked Judith eagerly after Mrs O'Donnell and Bill had exchanged greetings.

"Tell them!" ordered Nuala.

Bill then repeated to Judith and Mrs O'Donnell what he had just told Nuala about Anne Beatty and her conversation with Dr Waldron.

The two girls looked significantly at each other. "We thought as much," said Nuala grimly. "It's got to be something to do with that passage and the hole in the wall."

"Nuala had her suspicions that something would happen tomorrow, as it's the last day of term and everyone will be out of the way," reported Judith to a deeply interested Bill and Mrs O'Donnell.

Nuala's mother asked a little fussily, "What has Dr Waldron done? Is he really mixed up with those terrible women? Oh, Nuala, you haven't got yourself involved with them again? Once was more than enough. I don't know how I'll be able to break it to your father."

Nuala wasn't impressed. "That's isn't like you, Mum. You know Dad loved telling everyone about them last time. He used to call them the Wicked Ladies of the Boyne," she said.

Bill laughed. "Poor Mrs O'Donnell. Don't worry. I would be surprised if Dr Waldron has had anything to do with St Brigid's but I have to find out about this secret passage in the school. I am determined to find the way in or burst."

"Where's Nurse Beatty?" asked Judith.

Bill looked a bit embarrassed. "She couldn't come. She has a date with a police detective this morning; actually it concerned Dr Waldron too."

"But they'll never catch him," said Nuala, "He's on his way to New York!"

Bill smiled. "Don't forget that the plane stops for an hour at Shannon and then there's the fog. He might not find it so easy to get away."

"What's Nurse Beatty telling the police about the doctor?" asked Judith.

"I don't suppose I should tell you: so keep it to yourselves. She has reason to believe that he was blackmailing patients in St Winifred's Clinic. That's why she pretended to be friendly with him. Apparently, he would put them to sleep with a truth drug and then he would find out all their secrets. The worst part for the patients was that they wouldn't remember a thing when they woke up again."

"You're lucky, Judith, that you've no guilty secrets," laughed Nuala. "He gave you your anaesthetic, if you remember."

"How do you know I haven't?" said Judith with a grin.

"I think I'll push off to the school now," said Bill. "If he was telling the truth, I want to be around when the Wicked Ladies of the Boyne appear."

Nuala came to a swift decision. "I'll come with you. I know where the hole is. Mum, will you explain to Judith's parents and say how sorry I am to miss the presentation, if I'm late."

Poor Mrs O'Donnell could only gape at Nuala, but before she could say anything, Judith burst out with, "What do you mean, Nuala? I'm going too. I wouldn't miss it for all the tea in China."

"Don't worry, Mum," said Nuala. "We'll be perfectly safe with Bill. I am only dying to catch the countess. When I think of all she put us through last year! You will let us go, won't you, and explain it all to the O'Briens. Please, Mum, please!"

"I'll take good care of them, Mrs O'Donnell. I don't think we'll catch anyone but I would like them to show me the famous hole in the wall. I'll probably have them back before three." Bill's voice was reassuring.

Mrs O'Donnell looked at the two pairs of eyes beseeching her and weakened. She had got to know Bill well the previous year and knew he could be trusted.

"Very well," she said at last. "I hope the O'Briens will understand. Please, girls, be careful and hurry back. If you're too late, stay in the school and we'll pick you up this evening, although it's a great shame to miss such a big occasion."

Nuala hugged her mother. "You're the brillest, Mum, but you needn't worry, you know. Aileen, Josie and the twins are watching Major Gobberletts like hawks all day so we will be quite safe."

Strangely enough, Mrs O'Donnell, wondering what had come over her to let them go and watching them rush out of the building, wasn't particularly relieved by Nuala's parting remark.

At the same time as Bill Crilly's car left the airport and started its journey to St Brigid's, an angry woman stormed out of Jury's Hotel in Dublin. Calling a taxi, she gave an address in Ballsbridge. Ten minutes later, she burst into her flat where the angry flood of words which had been burning on her tongue since she left the hotel dried on her lips. "What goes on, Jo?" she cried. "Why are you dressed in those clothes and carrying suitcases?"

Jo put two cases down on the floor and silently handed a letter to the other woman. Looking puzzled, the countess opened the folded page and read:

Dear Jo,

By the time this reaches you, I will be 40,000 feet above the Atlantic, eating my lunch. Last year was a fun year but I think it's time I took my work seriously; so I have accepted a job in the US. By the way, I thought I would spare you the bother of smuggling the paintings out of the country and haggling with dealers. I can do this in New York, so last night I decided to take them with me.

You looked so peaceful in your sleep, so like an innocent baby, that I didn't dare wake you up and tell you about my plan.

My love to all, especially Pat and the Countess.

Regards,

Ken

The letter fluttered to the ground. "The dirty pie-faced rat!" expostulated the countess. "He's double-crossed us! How did he get into the flat? My keys! He must have stolen my keys and had another set cut."

"Keep calm, countess." Jo spoke in her customary cool way. "I woke up early this morning and suddenly remembered Pat mumbling about lost keys last night so I looked in the safe and found the goods gone and that note in their place. So in the role of an FBI agent I tipped off the police. I told them that Ken was the leader of an international gang of art thieves."

A slow smile crossed the countess's face. "The double-crosser double-crossed! I like that. I'm only sorry I won't be there when the police find those Picassos in his suitcase. But, Jo, did they believe you?"

"Don't worry, my dear, I can be very persuasive. Go and get changed: we haven't much time."

"Give me five minutes. I've no desire to get caught.

You can be sure that creep won't keep anything from the police either."

"No doubt. When I think of all the months of hard work and expense we've put into this job and absolutely nothing to show for it, I could tear him slowly limb from limb."

Her tone was so cold and menacing that the countess shivered as she left the room.

20

Wall Wanderings

It was nearly two o'clock by the time Bill drove up the school avenue and parked outside the castle. Taking some ropes and a powerful torch from the boot of his car he hurried after the girls. They led the way through the school grounds and straight to the pit. When he reached the spot, Bill tied a stout rope securely to a nearby tree and swung himself down into the pit, which was very wet and muddy. Nuala followed him, but Judith decided to stay and keep watch in case anyone hostile chanced to come that way.

After ten minutes of pushing and shoving every part of the walls of the pit, Bill owned himself beaten. "I've gone through this before. I'm beginning to think it's not the entrance at all," he said bitterly to Nuala, who felt very depressed after all the excitement in the airport.

Judith came over and peered down. The vegetation around the pit was very lush after the mild winter. "An luck?" she called and then with a wild shriek came slipping and bumping down to hit Bill who, caught unawares, was knocked sideways against Nuala. This caused Nuala to fall backwards against the wall behind her, where she slid gently to the ground.

Their lamentations and reproaches were cut short by a strange noise. Nuala looked behind her and shouted. "Look, look, Bill, the wall is moving!" Sure enough, one of the large stone slabs that formed part of the wall was moving slowly outwards, revealing a dark cavern within.

"Well, I like that!" commented Bill ruefully. "After all my efforts, it was opened by accident!"

Nuala and Judith picked themselves up, completely forgetting any bruises or injuries they might have sustained, not to mention the appalling green stains all over their best jeans. Bill shone his torch into the black space and went forward, followed by the excited girls. The entrance was very low but beyond it, the cavern opened out into a large area.

Bill shone his torch around and exclaimed, "There's a lot of fallen stones here. Somebody has been trying to get something out from behind them." He knelt down and rooted around in the dust and gravel. Then with a triumphant shout he produced something which he examined carefully in the torch light. "It's a ring, maybe gold!" he said finally.

"Now we know why she was always popping out of [illegible]," observed Nuala. "She must have been trying [illegible] all the loot from under the rocks!"

"It looks as if she's got away with it then," a disappointed Judith pointed out, "if Bill could find only one ring there!"

"That's probably why we never saw her, not even once this term," agreed Nuala.

Bill leant against the wall to help himself get up from the floor. As he did so the entrance slab moved rapidly, closing them in. The girls jumped with fright and Bill swore as he dropped the torch. "I think we should get out of here fast," he muttered as he picked up the torch again, "It's a dangerous place. There might even be another rockfall." Luckily the torch wasn't damaged.

He shone it around the cavern and said, "Look: there's the way up." Nuala and Judith looked in the direction of the light. They could see the first steps of what looked like a very narrow stone staircase in the back wall of the cavern.

Bill fumbled in his jeans pockets and produced a small torch, which he gave to Nuala. "I'll go first. You take this and bring up the rear," he remarked. "And remember, whatever happens, stick together. I don't want to have to tell your mothers that you're lost somewhere in the walls of St Brigid's! They would take it big, very big!"

Nuala and Judith laughed and the terrible feeling of panic which had swept over them when the entrance closed began to recede.

Bill picked his way carefully through the piles of

rubble on the floor as he led Judith and Nuala towards the exit.

They had hardly mounted a dozen of the rough steps of this stairway cut in the thick wall when Nuala, who was in the rear position as arranged, heard a series of dull thuds. They seemed to be coming from the cavern which they had just vacated. She stopped and looked behind her, flashing her torch as she did so.

The staircase was so narrow she couldn't see much at first, just thick clouds of dust that billowed up towards her.

As the dust settled she was puzzled by a sound as if sacks of coal were been emptied rapidly near her; then she realised with horror that the entrance from the cavern was completely blocked with rocks and stones.

"Bill, Bill!" she screamed in terror, as she turned and tried to catch up with her companions.

"Nuala, what's the matter?" Bill's anxious voice reached her. "Are you all right?"

Nuala bumped into Judith and clutched her thankfully. "Bill, there must have been another rock-fall back there," she explained in a trembling voice. "The stairway is completely blocked off with rocks and stones. How will we ever get out again?"

Bill looked at the two white faces straining up at him in the torchlight. He spoke briskly. "Don't worry, kids. You know there's a couple of exits in the castle itself. We'll find them. Come on; follow me."

His quiet, confident voice reassured them. They

fell in behind as he started climbing the steps again.

It seemed hours later to Nuala, though her watch showed that it was only twenty-five past two, when Bill stopped in a long, narrow passage. They must have climbed hundreds of steps, she thought, all on a kind of gently curving staircase, which was leading them they knew not where. It was a relief to be on the level at last.

"Come nearer, Nuala and Judith," said Bill in a voice of suppressed excitement. "I've found a peephole here. Do you recognise that place?" He moved over to let Nuala look first. Nuala put her eyes to a kind of slit in the wall and peered through.

"It looks a bit like the chapel corridor," she said finally. "What do you think, Judith?"

"I am inclined to think you're right," Judith agreed. "But it's very hard to tell from here."

Bill shone his torch up and down the walls and gave an exclamation. "Look up there, there's a kind of lever. Pull it," he cried.

Nuala immediately stretched up and fumbled at the lever. It was quite stiff but it eventually moved. There was a kind of clicking sound and slowly a narrow opening appeared in front of them. "It *is* the chapel corridor," said Nuala. "But she always came through the dormitory corridor!"

Bill was about to comment on this, when they heard a noise that sounded like someone shuffling along above them or perhaps ahead of them. Then there was a loud thump as if something heavy had fallen above them. It seemed that they weren't the only people wandering around in the walls of the castle. "Nuala," whispered Bill, "see if you can get out through that gap and run down for help. There could be at least three of them up there. Meet us in the dormitory corridor. We'll go ahead and watch from the rear."

Nuala just managed to squeeze herself through the narrow opening, realising why the intruder never used it. She fell out on the floor of the corridor. Picking herself up, she ran off as fast as she could. Then she heard a click and knew Bill had closed the wall behind her.

Sr Gobnait was gratified when a group of third-years approached her and asked her to come and watch the presentation with them in the common room. Aileen and Josie, who were at the back of this idea, were pleased by her acceptance, Aileen going so far as to select an armchair and put it in a place of honour for her. However, when Sr Gobnait arrived, she expressed a preference for the couch, so Aileen promptly sat in the armchair herself, whispering to Josie, who was perched on its arm, that it was a terrible pity Nuala wasn't there to see how faithfully they had carried out her wishes.

To the relief of those present, the programme on the paintings of the National Gallery had been quite interesting. It was over just before three o'clock. The cameras then switched over to the Long Room and soon all the third-years were watching the arrival of the VIPs with anxious interest, hoping to pick out Nuala and Judith from amongst them.

A few minutes later, Sr Gobnait was called to the phone. She rose, promising to return as soon as possible. Aileen gave Josie a nudge and they slipped out of the room closely followed by the twins. They walked slowly up towards the office, and were in time to hear her put the phone down.

As she came out of her office, a dishevelled figure in stained jeans and filthy jumper erupted down the stairs. "Aileen, Josie, Twins," it shouted. "Come quickly, Bill's in the wall and he needs help!" and then it dashed up the stairs again.

Aileen looked at Josie. "If I didn't know that she was in Dublin, I'd say it was Nuala."

Josie replied, "Look, there's Sr Gobnait going up the stairs; quick, follow her. Watch her like a hawk!" She ran quickly after the nun; Aileen and the twins weren't far behind.

As soon as Nuala was safely through the wall, Bill had pulled the lever again. Then, leading the way, he crept very quietly along the passage and up another flight of stone steps, followed by Judith. When they reached the top, he turned off his torch. As they turned the corner, they found that the passage ahead was illuminated by a strong beam of light coming from a different torch.

Bill could see a shadow of an arm stretching up to something on the wall, which he guessed was another lever. Judith, hardly breathing, followed as he crept towards the light, keeping close to the wall.

Meanwhile Nuala, having delivered her call for help, raced back up the stairs, two at a time, and ran down the dormitory corridor. Sr Gobnait and her watchers, making good time, weren't far behind her. Nuala, passing the window, slowed down for a minute and then went back and dragged the curtains across it. She gave a satisfied nod and pulled Bill's torch out of her jeans pocket.

She walked towards the place in the wall where she judged the hole should be. When Sr Gobnait and the others arrived panting along the corridor, Nuala whispered, "Hush!" and motioned them to stand back. She was waiting for the click.

A minute later, she heard it. The wall opened slowly, revealing a wavering light from a torch held very low. Nuala waited until the intruder stepped out of the hole; then she beamed her little torch straight at where she thought the eyes should be. The intruder, heavily burdened by two bags and blinded by the torch, made a desperate effort to get back into the wall, only to find Bill and Judith blocking their way.

The intruder dropped the two bags and made a dash for freedom down the corridor, followed by Sr Gobnait, who in her determination to catch the villain threw herself forward and by a lucky chance managed to knock her down. Josie sprang to turn on the electric light. Then they saw Sr Gobnait, who was kneeling on the floor, holding down a masked figure!

Judith hopped out of the hole in the wall easily, but Bill, who was tall and broad, found it much harder to get through the gap. As he squeezed through, he inadvertently set off some mechanism. The wall jerked gently closed again when nobody was watching it.

They stood around Sr Gobnait and stared as she leaned forward and pulled the mask off her prisoner's face. To everyone's amazement, it was revealed as that of Mrs McGlade, the art teacher.

Nuala gave a gasp and looked at her watch. "Oh my God, it's after three and we've missed the presentation!" she lamented.

21

The Great Wind-Up

"Don't worry, Nuala," said Sr Gobnait, smiling at her. "We've a good fifteen minutes left!" The tall nun had been very impressed by Nuala's trick with the torch. "Mr Crilly and I will take care of Mrs McGlade, or whatever she calls herself, and you and Judith can join the other third-years in the common room and watch the presentation on television. I know it won't be the same but it will be something."

She stood up, and so did the other woman, as Sr Gobnait had a tight hold of her arm. "My name is Pat McGlade," said the art teacher in a cold voice of fury. "Take your hands off me; I have done nothing wrong."

Sr Gobnait looked down at her. "I wonder," she asked sternly, "what you would consider wrong. We caught you breaking into the castle by a secret entrance and wearing a mask. It's not the first time either, by all accounts."

During this interchange, Aileen's curiosity, which

had been aroused by the sight of the two heavy bags which Mrs McGlade had dropped, overcame her. She bent down and started opening the one nearest her.

Bill looked from one woman to the other. "Do you want me to get the police?" he asked Sr Gobnait.

Before she could answer, Aileen's voice rang out: "These bags are full of gold coins and jewellery—piles and piles of it!"

Pat McGlade found her voice. "Those bags are full of treasure which I discovered by accident, when I was exploring the pit and entrance to the old escape route from the castle. Naturally, I was going to hand it over to the proper authorities. In fact I was on my way down to tell you all about it, sister, when I was attacked and brutally assaulted. As for the mask, it was merely my scarf, I pulled it over my face to keep it clean from all the dust in the walls there."

She spoke in a cold, superior voice and then glared disdainfully at them. In the shocked silence which greeted this bold speech, Sr Gobnait, looking thoughtfully at the girls and Bill, came to a quick decision.

"Perhaps you're right," she observed. "We'll go down to my office. I shall take care of the treasure. Then you can write down what you have just said to us and sign it. Mr Crilly and I will witness your signature. Then you can go. I don't want any scandals in St Brigid's. We had enough bad publicity last year."

Sr Gobnait then led Bill and Mrs McGlade down

the stairs, followed by the six third-years, who felt strangely cheated by the whole episode. When they had all reached her office, Sr Gobnait signalled to the girls to run off and try to catch the television programme before it was too late.

They arrived rather breathless in the common room just as Dr Beverly-Morrissey finished his speech. Josie and Aileen squeezed into an armchair. The others flung themselves down on the floor and leaned back against Josie and Aileen, who were sitting behind them.

Dr Beverly-Morrissey stepped forward and pressed the button which operated the curtains veiling the Picassos. Immediately they swished gently back across the wall, revealing the long-awaited McMahon legacy.

The loud clapping which had started up when the curtains began to move petered out quickly and a great gasp of dismay rose from the large crowd of notables present.

"I don't understand," Gwendoline cried out. "The middle picture is a view of St Brigid's. Nobody ever told me that Picasso went to school here!"

Nuala and Judith scrambled up from the floor. "It's my missing painting of St Brigid's!" Judith screamed excitedly. "Look, everybody! Look!"

Nuala screamed back at her. "Quick, Judith! Quickly, come with me to Sr Gobnait. Let's hope that we're in time to stop that art woman getting away from the castle. They must have switched the paintings—all three of them!" And both girls ran quickly from the common room.

When they reached the office, Sr Gobnait was carefully reading something written on a sheet of foolscap paper. Beside her stood Mrs McGlade looking haughtily through Bill, who was plainly unhappy. Nuala stood and barred the doorway. "Don't let that woman go, sister!" she called urgently. "She's just robbed the National Gallery!"

"What ever are you talking about?" asked a startled Sr Gobnait.

"It's true," corroborated Judith, standing beside Nuala. "We have irre...irrefutable evidence." She got the word out, feeling very pleased with herself.

"When Judith's cousin unveiled the paintings they weren't the right ones!" explained Nuala. "The middle one was in fact a view of St Brigid's that Judith painted last term!"

Judith pointed at the thunderstruck art teacher. "Only she could have taken it; it's been missing for weeks!"

The strident ringing of the phone interrupted them. A strained Sr Gobnait picked it up and then passed it to Bill. "It's for you, Mr Crilly."

Bill took it over and spoke into it. "Yes, Bill Crilly speaking." He listened intently for a few minutes, saying yes at intervals, and once no. Then he put the receiver back in its place.

"That was Anne Beatty," he informed them, a trifle self-consciously. "She says that the police got a tip-off about who switched the Picassos in the gallery. They are on their way down to Shannon now to pick up Dr Waldron. It appears that he and a few women accomplices did the job."

A queer gasping sound came from the art teacher. "They made me do it. I never wanted to do it!" She collapsed against Sr Gobnait, sobbing and howling. "They promised to get my husband, Fursey O'Hare, out of prison if I co-operated. Now he'll never get out!" Suddenly she rose and clutched Bill's arm. "Don't let them take me away," she pleaded. "I'll tell you everything I know. Here's their address for a start." She pulled a piece of crumpled paper out of her pocket and pressed it on Bill, who raised his eyebrows at Sr Gobnait, then took up the phone and started dialling quickly.

Sr Gobnait gave a sudden start. "Glory be to God!" she cried. "The hole in the wall. Judith, fetch the head girl and the prefects at once. Nuala, run around and tell each year that no one is to leave the common rooms until I send word to them. I don't want anyone going into that passage and breaking all their arms and legs."

As Nuala and Judith ran off to do the nun's bidding, they could hear Bill reading an address in Ballsbridge out over the phone. He was speaking to the police, they guessed. "That's great," Judith gloated to Nuala. "They won't get away with it. This time, they'll be caught."

"I hope so," agreed Nuala. "But imagine! Married to Fursey O'Hare. I can't believe it. I always thought he fancied the countess. It looks as if we'll be getting a new art teacher next term."

"I suppose so," replied Judith. "Do you think that that was her house last year; you know, the one Fursey locked us up in, in Connemara?"

Nuala nodded her head. "It must have been," she said. "Here's where we split. See you later in the common room." And she went off to the right as Judith went into the sixth-years' room, to tell the head girl and the prefects that they were wanted by the Major.

While these stirring events were going on in the school, fate had been catching up with Kenneth Waldron. Just as flight EI706 was about to leave Shannon Airport, Ken, who was deep in conversation with an attractive woman in the next seat, felt a soft tap on his arm. Looking up, he heard the pleasant voice of the flight attendant say: "Would you mind, please, stepping to the back of the plane, doctor? Someone wishes to speak to you."

Ten minutes later the plane took off for New York, but Ken Waldron hadn't resumed his seat. He was too busy trying to explain to the police what three valuable paintings belonging to the National Gallery were doing in the false bottom of his suitcase. His arrival back at Dublin Airport in police custody coincided with the departure of the early evening flight to Rome.

The flight attendant of this particular plane, who had welcomed aboard with great respect a tall, dignified bishop and a companion priest, who might have been his secretary, would have been puzzled if she had overheard their conversation about an hour later, as the plane flew smoothly southwards.

"Did you notice someone at Dublin Airport?" asked the priest. "A medical person we both know, looking quite shattered and accompanied by two very obvious-looking police detectives!"

"I did, countess, and I am glad to find that the Irish police were efficient in catching that particular thief," was the bishop's cool reply. "The FBI plan worked perfectly, though it's a pity about the pictures. Now what about a little drink to celebrate?"

The flight attendant passed drinks to the two supposed clerics and asked brightly, without waiting to hear their reply,"On your way to see the Pope, are you?"

The countess sipped her drink and relaxed comfortably back in her seat. "Yes, indeed," she murmured softly. "We must call on the Pope, when we get to Rome, and see if we can liberate a few of the paintings in the Vatican—to make up for our great disappointment in Ireland, of course!"

It wasn't late when Sr Gobnait allowed all the girls out of the common room, for when she and the prefects went up to see what they could do about the hole in the wall, they couldn't find it anywhere.

Later that afternoon, Josie, Aileen, Judith and the twins sat in their favourite tree waiting for Nuala to join them. When she clambered up beside them, they could see that she was looking very pleased about something. "Hi, chucks!" she said. "Sorry for being late, but I met Bill and managed to get the whole story from him."

"Go on, Nuala," Josie chivied her. "Start talking!"

So Nuala began. "The story started really last year, when Fursey, anxious to hide a few jewels away, accidentally stumbled across the hidden entrance to the secret passage. He hid them there, and when he was sent to prison, he told the whole story to his wife, one Pat McGlade. So she got a job in the school and started looking for the passage."

"Why didn't she just go to it?" asked Aileen. "Didn't Fursey tell her where it was?"

"I don't know about that, but she told Bill that it was really Judith's drawing of the pit which gave her the clues she needed. She found the entrance, but to her horror there had been quite a heavy fall of rock in the cavern and it took her weeks to find the jewellery and also a bag of gold coins which Fursey knew nothing about."

"He mustn't have been the only one who tried to put a bit away for a rainy day!" observed Eithne.

"We frightened her away at Christmas, when we tackled Sr Gobnait under the mistaken impression that she was the intruder. Then the countess and Jo O'Leary, who didn't know a thing about the treasure, persuaded her to paint the fake Picassos and give them a hand at switching the paintings."

"The poor thing," sympathised Judith. "She must have been driven mad by the lot of them. No wonder she mixed up my painting of St Brigid's with the Picassos!"

"I wouldn't worry about her; she was very quick to split on the others," Nuala said cynically.

Josie, who had followed Nuala's story with great interest, asked: "Did the police catch the countess and Jo O'Leary?"

Nuala shook her head. "When the police raided the flat, not only were they gone but they didn't leave a clue behind them. I don't know how they do it but they've completely disappeared."

"Just like last year," Aileen pointed out. "Maybe they were aliens after all!"

Nuala laughed. "I bet they are. That means they'll probably beam down again in search of earth treasures!"

"It occurs to me," observed Judith thoughtfully, "that even if they had been in the flat, the police wouldn't have caught them. They are such masters of disguise, as we know."

"You're right, Ju," agreed Josie fervently. "Remember, I didn't recognise the countess in that black curly wig, and I saw enough of her last year. The police hardly know what she looks like."

"Don't worry," replied Nuala carefully in an expressionless voice. "Bill told me that the police are aware of all that, so they have plain-clothes detectives stationed at all the ports, and every nun travelling abroad this week will be scrutinised carefully before she is allowed to leave the country."

They all stared at Nuala. Then Josie broke the silence with peals of uncontrollable laughter. The twins joined in and soon they were all infected with mirth. For several minutes the branches of the tree swayed with their paroxysms.

"Every nun will be scrutinised carefully," Josie repeated, wiping her eyes and still chuckling. "What a story! How do you think of them, Nuala?"

"It's not a story," denied Nuala indignantly. "That's exactly what he told me. It's true. He begged me not to tell the Major, as he thought that it might upset her."

"Poor Bill," sympathised Josie. "He's probably afraid she'll go to the EC about it and he'll be dragged into it."

"I guess you're right, chuck," replied Nuala. "As he dashed out to his car, he muttered something about accepting that job in Mexico after all."

Sr Gobnait's voice floated up to them from the river bank. Josie peered through the light canopy of pale green leaves. "There are two teams racing on the river. Gosh, these teams are really good," she called admiringly.

There was a scramble to look through the branches. "Wow!" said Judith. "They're really improved, aren't they?"

"You bet," answered Josie happily. "You've got to hand it to the Major; she may not be as good as Miss Keane at hockey but can she coach rowers!"

Nuala leaned back against the trunk of the tree.

"What a surprise in store for Newgrange Coll," she gloated. "I am only dying to see their faces when St Brigid's flashes past them in the boat races next term."

Also by Poolbeg

The Hiring Fair

By

Elizabeth O'Hara

It is 1890 and Parnell is the uncrowned king of Ireland. But thirteen-year-old Sally Gallagher, "Scatterbrain Sally" as her mother and young sister Katie call her, has no interest in politics. She is happy to read books and leave the running of the house to those who like housework.

A shocking tragedy changes the lives of the sisters. Instead of being the daughters of a comfortable Donegal farmer and fisherman, they have to become hired servants, bound for six months to masters they don't know.

Elizabeth O'Hara has written an exciting story that has its share of sorrow and joy. She creates in Scatterbrain Sally a new and unforgettable Irish heroine.

Also by Poolbeg

The Secret of Yellow Island

By

Mary Regan

The spirits of the past have risen at last to do battle with the spirit that is ageless – the spirit of evil.

When Eimear Kelly arrives in Donegal to spend the summer with her eccentric granny Nan Sweeney she is not prepared for the adventure about to unfold.

Who is the frightening giant of a man Eimear christens 'the Black Diver' who has rented her gran's holiday cottage? What is his dark secret and why is he poking about the deserted island of Inishbwee?

When Eimear meets Ban Nolan, a mysterious old woman, and discovers the legend of the Spanish sea captain, she is drawn into many exciting and dangerous encounters.

The Secret of Yellow Island is a story of a strange and unforgettable holiday.

Also by Poolbeg

The First Christmas

By

Michael Mullen

Daniel is ten and loves Christmas. He is a great friend of John Duffy, the local carpenter who carves the figures for the village crib.

One night before Christmas Daniel steps inside the crib and finds himself in Bethlehem just before the birth of the Christ child. He meets the shepherds and the Magi and is placed in mortal danger by Herod's murdering soldiers...

Michael Mullen has retold the world's best-known story with humour, freshness and excitement.